Shrinking Violets

Shrinking Violets

Heidi Greco

QUATTRO BOOKS

The publication of *Shrinking Violets* has been generously supported by the Canada Council for the Arts and the Ontario Arts Council.

 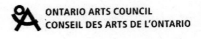

Cover photo: John Calabro
Cover design: Diane Mascherin
Author photo: George Omorean
Typography: Grey Wolf Typography
Editor: Luciano Iacobelli

Library and Archives Canada Cataloguing in Publication

Greco, Heidi
  Shrinking Violets /Heidi Greco

ISBN 978-1-926802-36-7

  I. Title.

PS8563.r41452s 2011   C813'.6   C2010-907656-7

Novella Series #19
Published by Quattro Books Inc.
89 Pinewood Avenue
Toronto, Ontario, M6C 2V2
www.quattrobooks.ca

Printed in Canada

For J and J and the lost boy

"In dog years I'm dead."

— *Unknown*

One.

February 2, 1990. That's what the header on the newspaper says. Still a new decade, but one that's already feeling tired. Half the world has just shrugged off its chains and here she sits, starting to feel the weight of her own.

As she pours herself another coffee, Reggie wonders if the groundhog has seen his shadow. And if he has, whether that means spring will come soon. Although really, she thinks, bending again to the crossword, who could put their faith in a rodent.

Twenty-eight down: A six-letter word for protrusion.

It can't be 'growth'. The R is in the wrong space. But then, maybe the word crossing it is wrong. Still, 'strains' or maybe 'sprains' are the only words she can think of that fit that clue: *results of violent exertion*.

She puts the pencil down and looks out the window.

It isn't that Randy's a bad guy. He's got lots of friends, is always being asked to parties. He just doesn't seem to like his women getting fat on him. Not even when they're carrying his baby.

She knows he'll be home from work soon, and she still hasn't started supper. He's been crabby enough since she's had to quit her job – since the manager told her she'd be "better off" at home. Reggie knew the truth: her hugely pregnant belly was making customers nervous about coming to her check-out. She knows that quitting has meant she'll have to go back to work sooner, that her pogey will run out a little faster. That's all.

Or that's almost all. It also means she'll have more time at home with him – just the two of them being a couple on their own.

She hopes that when the baby comes, and she can slim back down to her old self, he'll start being nice to her again. But considering everything he said last night, she isn't sure now whether that will ever happen.

And today, she hasn't even been able to go out because of the damn bump on her forehead. Too bad she'd gone and trimmed her bangs so short the other day, they might have helped camouflage the bruise. But when he'd told her she looked like a fucking sheepdog, she'd done what she could to improve things.

She rubs the mound of her belly through the tightly stretched T-shirt, avoiding the sensitive navel, wondering how much longer the baby can stay in there before her belly button explodes. She pictures it popping off, flying across the room, landing with a splash in somebody's bowl of soup, like a fly in a cartoon.

She knows she'll have stretch marks afterwards, another thing that probably won't thrill him. Once upon a time, he'd loved her 'perfect body'. She remembers how, laughing and half-drunk, he'd made his voice all raspy, rubbed his penis between her breasts, and croaked in a Leonard Cohen sort of way that he loved 'her pale white body with his mind.' Asked if she would always love his little mind. Then stuck his little mind in her mouth and gone on singing while she was supposed to hum along.

She heads for the bathroom to take yet another piss. Tries to think of something for supper that will put him in a good mood. Eases down onto the toilet seat, pulling down her pants. Lets go the driblets of pee into the bowl – all she can hold these days. She sighs and then the word for the puzzle appears, popping into her head from God knows where: 'hernia'.

◆

Randy manages to make it to the hospital, though not in time for the delivery. He's had to stop at the pub and brag it up to some of the boys. He's brought a slew of flowers though, along with a huge stuffed toy, a turquoise rabbit with scraggly pink ears and googly, mismatched eyes. It looks like something you might win at a carnival. Nearly twice as big as the baby, it's probably dangerous. Even on its own, the rabbit won't fit inside the plastic infant bed that stands beside Reggie's.

Randy is still chomping on a big cigar, but at least he has the sense not to fire it up in the hospital. Reggie nearly turns her head from his breath when he bends over to kiss her. "Hey, Carrot Top, ya done good, eh. Now when you gonna get home so I can have some of that beautiful ass."

◆

Reggie can see that Randy hasn't understood how flabby she'd be after the birth, stretched out and still so soft of belly.

Randy also doesn't like the way the baby cries so much, especially the way he seems to start up nearly every night at almost exactly 4 AM. Sometimes, no matter what Reggie does for the baby, it seems he can't stop crying. She even tries feeding him milk in a bottle, in case he isn't getting enough at breast.

This is the single best pleasure in all this chaos since the birth. Reggie loves the deep pulling sensation that comes with every suck at her nipple. How the sight of his little mouth gasping towards her makes the milk come rushing up into the front of her breasts, makes them harden, so nice and big for once in her life. And when the baby sucks, how she feels the pleasure of the pull so very deep inside.

She loves the way she can ease back with the baby, resting him on her arm. Close her eyes, relax, and simply be.

◆

There is a monster at the window. I can hear him, but I can't see him. I ask myself what kind of creature could climb as high as the seventh floor. I listen to his breathing, low and steady – a guttural purr. I consider ways I might sneak from the bed, crawl out the bedroom door. Only I know that the hallway is blocked, that escape is impossible. All I can do is hold my breath, be still enough that he won't know I'm here.

But his breathing grows louder, so I know he's getting closer. Trying to make a decision about who he will eat today.

When I see a blur outside the glass, I think he must be going to another window, another apartment, and feel a little rush of mean relief. But then I see his eye, and it is so watery blue, and his skin is blue and so is the sky. And I see that he has long ears but that he is a tyrannosaur, holding up his little hands, waving limply.

And then his mouth is in the room and his breathing is so loud, grunting and snorting in my face. He curls back his lips in a smile of recognition, showing his yellowed buck teeth. He smells so bad that when I try to scream, I choke.

"What the fuck?! What's the matter with you! If it isn't the fucking kid making noise, it's you."

And he shoves Reggie out of the bed and onto the floor with a sweep of his leg. She lands with a thump that's audible, and the baby starts to cry.

◆

Seventeen across: *winning character, Mary Poppins.*

Julie fucking Andrews doesn't fit the spaces. Dick Van Dyke's skinny butt would fill the squares all right, but his letters are wrong for the two she is sure about.

Reggie knows she looks a mess, and that the place does too. It's just too damn hard to get enough rest and still finish everything that has to get done. If only she could sleep for a single round of eight uninterrupted hours.

If Randy's around when the baby is asleep, he wants her to party, or at least keep him company while he does. She thinks, if only – if only there could be no Randy, no telephone, no buzzer, no baby. It's all beginning to make her crazy and she knows it.

At least Nickolas (she still can't get used to the name, it doesn't seem to suit him, but Randy has insisted) has fallen asleep on her arm. And as long as she doesn't move too much, she figures he'll stay that way for a while. It doesn't help with her own problems in the sleep department, but the quiet is certainly welcome.

She can see herself reflected in the window beside the kitchen table. Pretty shitty, all right. Randy is probably right to call her a dog. A bitch. A breeding bitch. That's all she's good for, he's told her again. And even then, poor Nickolas, her little baby dog-boy, he is going to be stuck with the same orange hair as hers. His started out blond and silky, but has been changing by the day. Still silky, to be sure, but clearly orange.

At least he has beautiful eyes. Dark like Randy's, bright and always moving. She thinks about Brian MacKenzie, her friend from when she'd been little, and wonders how long it took his mother to understand that her child's eyes didn't work, how long for her to accept the fact that they never would.

She tries to put herself into the mind of such a mother, who has to deal with a baby who is somehow less than perfect. One who has a shortened leg, a missing thumb, a mark across its body. Is it any less easy to love such a child? Or is it something, she suspects, that maybe makes you love them all the harder, all the stronger. As if by loving them more, you could maybe hold the world away. Or hold it back enough to give that child an even chance, the chance to live without any hurting.

But the thought of living without hurting seems like yet another symptom of her craziness. Sitting on the wobbly kitchen chair, she takes stock of her reflection in the window – hair uncombed, wearing a bathrobe with sour milk on its shoulder. She laughs – she has to – at the hopeless optimism of it all. And then picks up her pencil, printing in the blanks J-U-L-I-E-A-N-D-R-E-W.

She knows the answer is wrong – the star and even the spelling – but she figures maybe just a part of the ever-smiling Julie might be enough for the planet. Besides, if optimism doesn't want to fit into the squares, well, she is going to find a way to make it goddamn fit.

Two.

Nicky has just turned four and seems happy at his play-school. Reggie, still working at the Safeway, is reasonably content. Randy has long since disappeared, along with a fancy blonde girlfriend. One day he'd come home early from work, dragging the girlfriend along to the apartment. She was there supposedly to help him get his stuff, but Reggie is pretty sure that Randy brought her along just so she'd be able to see that he'd found himself somebody who was better looking than her.

The girlfriend had the sense at least to look embarrassed when all this happened, and Reggie could tell she hadn't known there'd be a baby. Oh well, he had given her half the next month's rent before he'd left. That was at least something – and in cash, too.

It has been a series of apartments and basement suites in the time between, but she has started to think about finding them a little house. One that has a yard where they could maybe keep a dog. One where they could put up a tent and pretend that they are camping. She knows that Nicky would love tenting out. She just knows it.

He loves it when she helps him build forts underneath the table, draping sheets and blankets to shroud them inside. And he loves it best when she moves their little television so the two of them can sit in the darkness there, eating popcorn and watching whatever is on.

The two of them are a unit, and she likes that a lot. Still, she sometimes wishes she could find him a dad. But then she remembers that he already has a dad, even though a lot of good it does either of them.

She has gone out with a few guys since Randy, but somehow, none of them have turned out to be important to her. Most of them have been fun, and the sex has usually been fine, but something is always missing. The Big Magic. Whatever. Who ever really knows what it all comes down to?

Nicky's having a lie-down and the afternoon feels lazy. She lights a cigarette and watches the smoke make its way upward. She knows it is a rotten habit and that it costs too much. But when she thinks of all the other things she doesn't get to do, well, maybe there are worse things in this world.

She opens the weekend paper, looking for the crossword.

When the big weekend puzzle turns out to be too hard, she lets her mind wander to her days with the MacKenzie family, finds she can almost replay the afternoon she'd first met Brian. He wasn't much older than Nicky is now. She can't have been more than six or seven herself. She remembers not even noticing anything different about him. But then something had happened – she'd tried to point out some squawking bird – likely a jay – and frustration had led her to accuse him of not being able to see. Then, the way he'd answered that, yes, that was exactly it – he wasn't able to see. And knew that something inside of her had changed that day.

She remembers him muttering that he'd been born blind, then thinks of when she'd leaned forward and tried looking into his eyes, to see what might have been different about them. Aside from not looking back at her, they'd seemed normal enough. And Brian so matter-of-fact about it, explaining that he'd be going off to blind school in a year. He'd sounded so proud of that, offering that you *had to be blind* to get to go there.

She even remembers wondering whether a school full of blind kids would be a kind of chaos. She pictured kids as they knocked into each other, rattling each other like so many bowling pins.

Best of all, she remembers the two of them laughing – one time with Brian shoving his arm out at her, punching her suddenly in the chest. But that it had felt good in a hurty kind of way, and that they'd thrown their heads back and probably laughed the rest of the afternoon. And then Nicky is in the room, asking her what's wrong, can they look at *Where's Waldo* so he can read to her.

She hugs him and kisses his eyes, to which he sputters and laughs that she is the silliest mother in the world.

Three.

Harmon is the new guy in produce at the Safeway, transferred in from someplace in Alberta. He has hands that mark him as a produce manager. He stacks up a load of grapefruits the way some handle mandarin oranges, and the pyramids he builds for displays withstand countless squeezings and choosings. He is well over six feet, dark-haired, and – if such a thing is possible – almost too handsome. Reggie hasn't been able to ignore his arrival. She's heard he left his wife not all that long ago, and figures that must be one of the reasons he's moved here.

She doesn't know why, but when he asks her out, she hesitates. Still, all he wants to do is go bowling and for pizza. It seems innocent enough, especially when he says sure, that Nicky can come too.

She surprises herself at the trouble she takes over what she should wear to go bowling, and even buys Nicky a new T-shirt. When Harmon arrives to pick them up fifteen minutes earlier than he'd said, he apologizes, says the place was "easier to find than he'd thought it would be." She feels slightly foolish, being so obviously ready, waiting for him to arrive, like some stupid girl ready for her grad date to show up. All that's missing are the parents with the camera. Thank God at least for some small favours.

Luckily, it's five-pin lanes he takes them to, though he tells her in the car that he usually plays ten-pin, that he's been in a mixed league, partners with his wife. Or his 'ex' as he corrects himself, obviously still learning.

She remembers how hard it can be, this getting over being with someone. Even someone you might not particularly like anymore. Where was it – somewhere, she had read such a hopeless description – that marriage was about two people, grown so dependent on living together that they endured, even though both of them only grew more bored and dulled by the other. Ugh. No wonder she still mostly enjoys being on her own. No wonder she doesn't take out one of those ads in the back of the paper, desperate-sounding: "Marry me. I'm the one for you."

Harmon is good with Nicky, and she wonders if he has many chances to see his own kids. She's heard that he has a couple of them, maybe a boy and a girl.

This 'hearing stuff' is one of both the advantages and drawbacks of going out with someone from work. Rumours are one of the reasons she's always avoided it, at least until now. She can't help but wonder about him, wants to learn some personal details, but feels hesitant to ask him, doesn't want to cause him any pain.

Harmon has his own bowling shoes, but rents pairs for Reggie and Nicky. His are quite normal, black and reasonably plain, except for the curlicue stitching in patterns across the top. The rented ones are hideous, made up of patches, all different colours.

They make jokes about how ugly the shoes are, promising they won't steal them, how they'll be sure to get their own back when they finish their games. Even the guy at the rental counter has to agree and laughs, "Yeah, not too many people try to steal our shoes."

Reggie watches Harmon help Nicky swing the ball back before releasing it and shows him how he'll find more strength using both of his hands, helps him take aim for the headpin in the middle, reminds him not to drop the ball onto the floor, please. He knows what he's doing around kids, that's for sure. She half-wonders what might have happened between him and his wife.

After, at the pizza place, she turns her brightest red, as most of the cheese slides off the piece she's holding while she's talking. It's fallen smack into her lap before she can do anything about it. Her white pants will never be the same. So much for sexy. Not that she's gone out of her way to look sexy, but sexy is part of what a girl does to look nice, and now she feels like such a slob, an idiot again.

Harmon is very helpful, and goes to fetch paper towels and a glass of club soda, telling her if it works on red wine, it should work on pizza sauce. Nicky thinks, of course, that all of this is hilarious. Mothers aren't supposed to spill. That's a job for kids. Or that's the story he tells several times, laughing at his own joke, all the way home in the car.

When Harmon takes them to the door, she asks him in for coffee, not exactly sure what's expected of her at this point. She isn't really used to this three-on-a-date thing. He smiles, tells her no thanks, and pats Nicky's head good-bye. Still, she feels like she owes him something. No, that isn't quite right. But darn, he's been nice to them. "Good night," she says, reaching up and touching the side of his face, "thank you, Harm."

"Harmon," he corrects her, turning and disappearing.

◆

It isn't the first time she's seen the mousey-looking little girl in the store, but it's the first time the girl has come to Reggie's check-out line. The shopping cart is pretty full, some big boxes of cereal, a bunch of Kraft dinners, a couple loaves of bread. Jam, a bunch of bananas, wieners, two cartons of milk. Coffee and peanut butter round out the order. As the girl finishes stacking the items on the belt, she looks straight into Reggie's face and asks for three packs of Export A Kings.

"I don't think you're old enough to be buying cigarettes."

Digging into the pocket of her jeans, she pulls out a ragged piece of paper, hands it over. "Here, I've got a note. They're for my mother."

The note is creased and nearly falling apart. Reggie looks at her and shakes her head, "Honey, you know we can't sell to kids – not even with a note."

The girl looks up and says in a voice that seems to come from someone much older, "C'mon. If I don't get some, she'll kill me." Reggie frowns and chews her lip, wondering what to do. The girl looks at her so steadily, gazing through those long brown bangs, that Reggie finally turns and bends to the rows of packs stacked behind her. "Here. I'll give you one. But don't ever ask me to do this again. I don't want to lose my job."

"One'll be okay," she says, disappearing the pack into her jacket like magic. "I'm not sure I've got enough money anyway."

Reggie totals the order and tells the girl the figure. She already has a fist of bills waiting. The money she hands over is almost exactly the right amount. Reggie only has to hand her back a few coins.

No one is waiting in her line, so she takes her time bagging the groceries, tries talking with the girl. "You're a pretty good shopper. How old are you anyway?"

"Eight and a half," the girl shoots back. "Almost nine."

"Are you going to need a hand with this? Should I get someone to help you outside to your parents' car?"

"Whaddya think the carts are for?" she scowls.

Reggie watches her leave the store and wonders where the girl's parents are. Who is this hard little girl, so capable and so tough-seeming? Could she herself have ever been anything like this?

Her reverie is interrupted by a flurry of movement as a few items start appearing on her belt. She turns and smiles to the customer, "Hello, and welcome to Safeway," but can't stop wondering about the girl with the messy brown hair.

◆

Reggie is on her break, sitting in the lunch room with Sylvia, one of the old-timers at the store. Sylvia is bitching again, but then, it seems she's always griping about something or other. Today it's lighters, child-proof lighters.

"What is it anyway, with these goddamn child-proof lighters? Why should someone as old as me have to be child-proofed anyways? I had all my kids and they're grown up and gone now. What do they think I'm gonna do, burn down the friggin' house?"

Reggie doesn't know Sylvia all that well, even if they've both worked at the store for a long time. The managers seem to try to be sure no one gets breaks together too often. Gloria always says it's so they won't compare notes, maybe then decide to get radical and go out on strike.

"Well, you have grandchildren, Sylvia, don't you? Don't you worry about them?"

"Hardly ever see 'em. If I'm lucky, I get school pictures at Christmas."

End of that argument. So much for trying.

"The government thinks they know so much and can tell us all how we should live. They always know better than regular people. I ask you, did anybody ever ask you if you wanted child-proof lighters? No, of course they didn't. That would be too democratic."

She's on a roll now. There's nothing to be done but let her finish her spiel. And from the practised sounds of this speech, she's given it a time or two before.

"I mean, if I have little kids around, sure, they're probably a good idea. Don't want the little buggers burning up the bedroom, eh? But who gets to tell me that I've got no choice, can't buy anything *but*. I mean, what if I've got arthritis? Like, then what? Rent me a kid? Hell, they're the only ones who can make 'em work in the first place. That's how stupid your average government schmuck rules are. Useless bastards."

With that, she seems to have purged herself, having stated her piece for the day. Sylvia butts her smoke and puts up her feet, leans her head back into the chair and lets out a sigh.

Reggie finishes her cigarette too and quietly leaves the lunch room. So much for asking Sylvia if she knows who the scruffy little girl is.

◆

There is a blue whale in the river. Only this odd freshwater whale is a truly bright blue, nearly turquoise against the brownish hue of the water. It is swimming up the river, chugging its tail up and down, speeding hard as a motorboat making its way against the current. I am thinking what fun it would be to water ski behind it. Feel the tug of the rope against the pull of my arms, go bumping over the wake, jumping the edges back and forth. Hair streaming back in the breeze of my own speed.

I am standing on the porch at somebody's summer cabin, looking out over the river, watching the bright blue whale do its motor cruise along the water. Someone else is staying here. It must be that we're sharing the cabin. She turns her blonde head and I recognize her face. It is Randy's girlfriend, the one who came and helped him when he took his stuff away from the old apartment.

I am stiff and shy about spending time with her, half-worrying that Randy will show up at any second. That he will call me a dog again and make me feel bad. But the blonde woman is very nice. She holds my hand while I stir a pot of stew. I smell her very close to me, feel her pillowy breasts so soft, leaning into my back, and think of her face with a bright orange moustache, smiling up from down there in the midst of my tangled orange hair.

The dream wakes Reggie, pulling her out of sleep. So vivid she can feel herself wet and engorged. This must be a message: too long since she has been with a man. She puts her hand between her legs and rubs until she comes, imagines herself shooting into the mouth of the blonde, both of them sprawled out, naked and hot in the afternoon sun, riding on the back of the bright blue whale.

◆

The phone rings. It is Harmon. She will not call him Harm again. Though she wonders who could name their son such a boring name. It is hard, in fact, not to think of him as a boring man. It is just his name, she thinks. He can't help his name.

Maybe she could learn to call him Darling or Pookie. The thought of either of these causes her to laugh. He stops what he is saying, and asks what is so funny.

"Nothing," she says. "Nicky's tickling my foot." Nicky is in fact building Lego in his room.

They arrange a date, this time dinner and a movie. Saturday. Can she get a sitter in only three days' time?

This sounds somehow serious. A warning she should maybe heed. Message in a fortune cookie. Beware the quiet venture.

Since the bowling and pizza-fest, the three of them have gone on several dates. Miniature golf, a nature hike, a picnic, more bowling. This is the first time he has asked her to leave Nicky at home.

Nicky seems very comfortable hanging out with him and she likes that part of knowing this man. And Nicky doesn't seem bothered a bit by Harmon's dorky name, doesn't seem to mind the lame jokes he repeats.

She tells him the plan sounds nice and that she'll see what she can do. Asks him to phone her back tomorrow after work, that she should know by then.

After she hangs up, she wonders if she is truly going out of her mind. Whether she should instead maybe go looking for the blonde.

Four.

Something about the blonde has made her think about high school. How different it was from elementary school. How there were so many different kids there to get lost in. And best of all, the way there were so many different things to do.

The art room had clay for pottery, not just paper, paint and crayons. And parts of Home Ec had been pretty fun. They'd been able to make T-shirts and then paint on their own designs. She had made a blue whale jumping up and out of the water. It didn't really look like the photo she'd tried to copy from the *National Geographic*. But it didn't look all that bad, and she'd worn the shirt regularly for weeks. Only then it had shrunk when her mother had mixed it into the dryer, complaining, "What good is a shirt if you can't even put it in the dryer?" Still, Reggie liked it enough that she wore it for sleeping anyway.

By the time she was fifteen, she even had a boyfriend. Ken liked taking engines apart, and amazingly to her, knew how to put them back together so they worked. He would tell her over and over about how he would have his own shop someday. Not have to work for somebody else, the way his dad did.

They spent a lot of time fooling around in the shed behind his house, fooling around with more than the cars out there. He taught her how to kiss, how to put her tongue into his mouth, the same way he did to her. Showed her how to hold him, make him shoot in her hand. Sticky, how she'd never quite be sure what to do with the mess. He always seemed happy when she did this for him, happier than she probably was doing it. It was mostly messy and a little embarrassing afterward, to be sitting around with his thing there, lying in her hand. How different it looked afterwards than when it was up and throbbing. How small and curled, she thought. Except for all the hair around it, like some animal from the sea.

Ken loved Reggie's hair, the way it was so orange, especially the hair that showed when she finally let him take off her clothes. She thought about the afternoon she'd let him put his face down into her hair. It had at first seemed weird that he would want to do this to her, 'go a-quinting' as he called it, use his mouth to kiss and suck at her. How he ever got the idea was crazy enough in the first place, but then boys were supposed to be strange, or at least a lot different than girls.

He'd laid her on a back seat he'd removed from one of the cars and taken off her panties, looking at the orange hair between her legs, saying how beautiful it was, touching just touching the insides of her thighs, until he was able to nudge her legs open. Reggie remembers that when he had first put his tongue there, how she'd pulled back. It had been like something electric. But Ken had soothed her and promised he'd be nice. Instead of putting his tongue there right away, he'd blown a cool stream of air. So thin and soft that when he kissed her again, she hadn't resisted, hadn't minded at all. In fact, it had felt so wonderful, she'd forgotten about it seeming weird, probably even pushed back against his mouth.

After the day she'd first let him do that, it wasn't very long until they'd made love, or as they'd thought of it then, 'did it'. 'It' had seemed a big deal, and Reggie had been afraid, but Ken had a way of making everything seem so natural. He'd seemed more like a man than a boy – the way he could fix things, was able to lift her in his arms. It had been so easy to pretend that she was his wife. Even though they both were still only in Grade Ten and hadn't yet taken Sex Ed Eleven. When he'd pointed this out to her, they'd both laughed. "Do you think maybe we'll be able to get an A?"

She could still remember, though, that the first time he'd jammed himself into her, it hadn't felt very wonderful. More hard and hurty than anything, hardly like the rapture they described in the romance books. But he'd sure seemed happy and, when there'd been a little blood, had helped her with a clean white handkerchief.

Blood had been something that had surprised her, as it had never been mentioned in the novels she'd read so carefully. He'd shown her how to hold the cloth tight on the spot where he'd torn her. Told her to wear it home and wash herself well. And then to tuck another clean one into her panties for the night.

She thinks about after he'd moved away, having quit school during that rainy September of their Grade Eleven, when he'd gone to live with his uncle in New Brunswick so he could work for him back there. How he'd written a batch of letters, but that by Christmas, they'd been finished with each other.

She considers the fact that he'd wanted to get married – as he'd called it, "getting on with real life" – and is grateful that she hadn't been ready to. Lucky thing she had known it and hadn't been afraid to tell him so. His letters had started off persuasively enough, saying he'd found a place for them, how he was going to fix it up for her, that she would love it, that sort of thing. But it wasn't so long afterward, his letters had changed, as if the conviction of his ardour was petering off. She'd known he'd probably found himself someone else to love. And although it had stung her for a while to picture his face down there, hidden in another girl's hair, secretly she'd been glad that he was gone and out of her life.

Relieved, too, that she'd never got pregnant out there in the shed, though by what miracle that had been, she would never know. Despite Ken's apparent knowledge of fleshly pleasures, he'd never mentioned anything about birth control. So at least there'd been a few things for her to learn in boring old Sex Ed. Still, Reggie remembered chuckling to herself as the teacher had droned her dried-out explanations of foreplay. She'd wondered if Miss Barnes had ever known the joys that she had known. Somehow, she doubted the possibility.

Five.

The girl with the messy hair has come into the store again. This time she is no-nonsense and in a hurry. Has a carton of milk in her hand, plunks it onto the belt, asks Reggie for a packet of smokes, "A pack of Export A Kings. Please."

Reggie shakes her head, makes a face that says 'go away', is afraid the man who's approaching her check-out will overhear while she whispers, "I can't!"

The girl pounds a pile of coins onto the counter, grabs the carton of milk, flashes a look of utter disgust, and runs for the door. If Reggie hadn't known better, she'd have sworn the girl looked like someone was going to tackle her and arrest her if she didn't get out of there fast. She looks after her, wondering what she could have done differently.

"Hello. Earth calling. Want to ring in my groceries?"

The customer brings her back, out of her reverie. But she'd still like to figure out what is going on with that kid.

◆

Harmon is at the door. It is Saturday night. He is taking her to a steak place and after to a movie, though they still haven't decided which one they'll see. Nicky's on the couch, jumping up and down, trying to make them promise they won't go see the latest Disney without him. Reggie laughs and promises, crossing her heart that they won't. She reaches for a kiss good-bye and Nicky jumps her way, nearly flying into her arms, the safety there.

He has already had his bath, his hair is still damp. It smells so sweet, deliciously of oranges. This even though it is supposed to be lemon-fresh shampoo. Must be the colour thing, she thinks inside herself. Loving him so hard sometimes, she thinks that she could burst.

One more time she reminds the sitter, Tess, where they will be eating, says that she'll phone later when they've decided what to see.

Nicky takes a running lunge, diving hard at Harmon's legs, hugs him above the knees and does a dance. Harmon grabs the skinny waist and lifts him upside down, shakes him side to side, Nicky shrieking with delight.

Reggie and Harmon can still hear his noise as they make their way towards the elevator. Reggie feels a twinge of guilt, thinking Tess will have her hands full.

Even though autumn has officially arrived, the night is unseasonably warm and sweet-smelling. Harmon takes her hand as they walk to his car. She tries to think of ways she might fit herself better to him. Even though he tells dreadful jokes, she believes he is a good man. Smiles as he holds the door for her, gets into the car.

They are quiet as they drive to the restaurant, but it is not an uneasy kind of stillness. The radio plays softly, something FM and relaxing. She could do worse than spend her life with a man named Harmon. Then the memory of an oldies' tune butts into her brain – Sue-somebody, cooing a song about someone named Norman – but of course, Reggie's mind has replaced that name with Harmon's.

But this thought breaks the peace of her mood, and Reggie starts to giggle. He looks over towards her, as if to ask what's so damn funny. But she just waves her hand at him, saying, "Nothing, nothing. It's just me." And understands already, she is lying to him.

◆

Sunday morning sees her drinking coffee, smoking endless cigarettes, and doing the big weekend puzzle. One of those challenging ones where something is out of the ordinary: the starred words have to go backwards or everything is punned. She thinks that she has maybe got it: they're written like headlines but the answers merge terms so they cross over each other. *Musical feline climbs Empire State*: 'The Lion King Kong'. This works well until she gets to *Russian tsar goes Hollywood tragic*. 'Peter the Great Gatsby' makes sense, only it contains too many letters. Somehow 'Pete the Great' – which would fit – doesn't sound regal enough. Still, mistakes have been known to happen, even in crosswords.

She tries this, printing quickly, but no, that doesn't do it. The letters intersecting the front of the name don't work. She knows it is stupid to waste her time at silly puzzles, but they give her an excuse to sit down, relax, and have a smoke. Besides, she kids herself, they are good for her brain. Goes to erase her answer but accidentally rips a jagged hole in the thin paper. Butts her cigarette and dumps the last of her coffee into the sink. Time to get her ass in gear. Harmon's coming over in an hour.

In the shower, she wonders just what it is that has been bugging her since last night. Dinner had been excellent. She had even managed to eat the meal without dropping food into her lap. Without any quibbling they'd found a so-so movie and talked about it afterwards, both of them agreeing that it didn't rate more than a six. He had been the perfect gentleman. Maybe, the thought nagged her, that had been the problem. Maybe she'd had so many Randys in her life that a nice normal Harmon just wouldn't do the trick.

Before Randy, there'd been Max. Actually Max had been there part of the same time as Randy. She felt a little ashamed of that now. It hadn't been fair to either of the guys, and she didn't think she'd tell Harmon about it. It had, as she remembered, been more than a little awkward, complicated in so many respects. It had involved a lot of lying and covering up for what she was doing, though there had been a wonderful kind of exhilaration with all that attention. The best was when she'd actually managed to sleep with both of them in a single day.

Yet looking back on Max and Randy, neither had been the kind of lover Ken had been for her. But then maybe, she thinks, it's just that your first love somehow seems the best − sweet and pure, but at the same time, new and exciting.

Ken had always been willing to take his time on her, lavishing his tongue, his nibbling teeth all over her body. She wondered sometimes how his parents had let them spend so many hours out there in the shed all on their own. Wasn't it obvious that, even though they were so young, they were clearly in love − in lust − with each other? What if one of his parents had decided to come out there and had found them? Her lying there, spread across a back seat, him all hard inside of her, banging away.

Would they have phoned her parents? Or would they have called in a preacher, made them get married on the spot? Somehow that seemed the more likely scenario. They had Jesus pictures and slogans of all varieties − painted, cross-stitched, carved, and engraved. There was even a wooden plaque with strangely inlaid writing − only those who were 'saved' could read the message. Some of them gave her the creeps, especially the one that hung on a nail in the wall out in the shed, a painting of Jesus surrounded by little children. She used to make Ken turn it around when she knew they were going to get sexy. He kind of liked that, she used to think. He knew it was a sign that she wanted him.

A chill in the water brings her back to the business of rinsing, but she can't help considering whether Harmon would have pictures of Jesus at his place, and she realizes that not only has she not seen where he lives, she doesn't even know what part of town he's in. Something about that realization makes her wonder why that is.

Dunking her hair for a final rinse under the shower, she listens as the water pounds away at her head, as if a good pounding might bring her some answers. As if a good pounding might be all her brain needs to make better sense of things.

In the other room, Nicky pounds at his Lok-Blox with one of Reggie's shoes. The blocks are sticking and don't want to go together. But he looks pretty sure that he can fix them if he tries.

Six.

Nicky is calling for her. She has fallen asleep on the couch. It seems he has spotted a spider in the bathtub. She tells him it can't hurt anything and to just leave it alone. But then he comes in to show her with his hand all spread out. "It's as big as this," he says to her. "With hairy stuff on its legs." This sounds like a serious spider all right, so she gets up and goes along with him to see it.

When she's seen it, all she can think to do is close the bathroom door, positioning the inch of hollow plywood as a barrier between them and it. But she realizes that, eventually, one of them is going to have to get back in there—if not for a bath, at least for something else.

Nicky looks into her face and asks if she is scared of it.

Not wanting to frighten him any more than he is already, she, of course, has to tell the Big Lie. "No, silly, of course I'm not. He's just a dumb old spider, not even as big as my hand. Why, I could crush him in a second, don't you think?"

Nicky does not look convinced—neither, she fears, does his mother. In fact, pretty well everything she's said has been a whopping lie. Maybe even the part about it not being as big as her hand. Thinking about this, it worries her more, and she considers various possibilities, from the broom to the vacuum to a can of Lysol spray.

She knows that the broom is too hit-or-miss, that if she misses on the first try, she might accidentally swoop it up and into one of their faces. She doesn't want to share this one. Doesn't think Nicky needs this particular horror story, especially not this late in the evening.

The vacuum cleaner seems too disgusting, or maybe just too unfair. Besides, she's afraid she'll electrocute herself. Lot of good that would do Nicky. Her dead on the bathroom floor, the spider still loose, and by this point probably climbing over the edge of the tub to feast on her already-cooling corpse. All right, imagination overload on that one. And Lysol probably won't do a thing to the spider, but make it wet and clean-smelling. No good.

Then Nicky gets an idea. "I know!" his eyes light up. "Let's phone Harmon. We can keep the door closed 'til he gets here. He'll know how to get it out so it can't hurt us."

Okay, here are fighting words. She can rise to these. Pushing up her sleeves, she looks at Nicky, "Follow me."

Together they search in the space beneath the kitchen sink, hunting for the biggest jar they can find. The thought crosses Reggie's mind that there might well be a spider in here too, but she shushes herself inwardly, never speaking the idea.

There is a big one from Cheez Whiz. Nice and tall, for sure, but narrow at the mouth, too narrow for capturing the big guy. Then a huge one from the giant jar of salsa that had lasted most of the winter. This will do the trick. Now, if only they could find its lid, but no such luck on that. In the end, they set out armed with the salsa jar and a lid from a margarine tub. Nicky has big eyes as she opens the bathroom door.

By then, of course, the spider has disappeared. Probably down the drain, or worse, into the folds of the shower curtain. Both of these thoughts remain unspoken. Reggie just tells Nicky that the spider has gone home, and since it's so late now, he doesn't have to take a bath tonight. "How about jumping into your jams and I'll make some hot chocolate. Then we'll drink it up and snuggle for a story."

Later, while Reggie is brushing her teeth, a flash of dark fur scurries up the side of the tub – a big enough blur to catch her eye. Big enough to make her glad such a huge jar of salsa had been on sale. Maybe because it's late, maybe because she's just so determined, the spider permits her to quietly entrap him in the glassy dome. The margarine lid slides in neatly between the tub's surface and the top of the jar.

She takes the closed jar out to the kitchen, places it on the table. To be sure that he'll stay put, she sets the sugar bowl on top of the lid, a serviceable-enough weight. Stands back and admires him, trapped in his private terrarium. Mission accomplished. Without an intervention from the boringly normal Harmon, the one whose name still matches the song that sticks sideways in her head. The man who, no matter how darn good-looking he is, is not going to end up being father to her child.

◆

It is getting harder to keep Harmon at bay. Especially where she always sees him at work, smiling at her from the produce department, standing there in his apron, arranging lettuces, pulling beetles out of the spinach like the nickels her corny uncle used to pull from behind her ear. She thinks about his hands – hands that handle cantaloupes and cucumbers and grapes. It was getting so she wanted to stop accepting the discount fruits he kept aside for her. The last bunch of bananas he'd given her had been mushy and soft. They'd made her think about his penis. Could it be that it was mushy too? Was that why his wife had left him? Dependency was such a shoddy thing.

Nicky always asks about Harmon, but since they'd caught the spider, she's been feeling more independent, more confident about being on her own. A simple thing really, trapping a poor stupid spider inside a big empty jar. Covering the top with a lid and watching the creature slip around on the inside of the glass. How safe it had felt to look at it, marvel at its hairy legs. Superior was the feeling. Superior beings, she'd thought at the time – that was them.

She recalls how when they'd finally tipped the jar, laying it down on the grass by the sidewalk, it had taken nearly a minute for the spider to see its chance, its opportunity for freedom, before it had scurried off. Reggie remembers noticing this hesitation, how she'd thought about it while she'd watched Nicky trail along behind it, following its crooked walk across the lawn. She remembers too how sunset-filled the sky had been when he'd announced that the spider had disappeared, and how good it had felt when he'd taken her hand so the two of them could go back inside.

Seven.

Reggie doesn't know exactly what it is that bugs her about Harmon. She knows she has some kind of prejudice against his name – understands that connecting it to that easy-to-get-stuck-in-your-head song probably has something to do with it. He is certainly nice enough to her. In fact, he is nice to everyone, keeps people smiling as they wander through the produce department. He's always ready with answers about when a fruit is ripe, ready too with the same tired jokes that keep the old ladies giggling. And Nicky sure seems to like him. But then, Nicky likes everybody. That's just the kind of kid he is.

And it seems stupid not to like a guy because of his name. That isn't something he can do much about. Not any more than old Brian MacKenzie could have done anything about being blind. That's just the way it was. But to Reggie, Brian's blindness was less of a problem than poor old Harmon or his name was getting to be. She couldn't help but wonder where Brian was now, anyway.

◆

I am in a tower of glass, looking at the street below. A man is carrying Nicky, he is taking him away.

The man is trying to put him into the pocket of his pants, but of course Nicky is too big for that, won't fit.

Yet, neat as a pancake, the man is folding Nicky, bending him over, square upon square, making him into a size that will fit his pocket like a hanky. Zooming through some dream lens, the glass walls enlarge the scene, and as I look below, I can see the man through the windshield of his car. As he pulls out of the parking lot, I can see his face. He is smiling. He is none other than Mr. Stale Jokes Harmon.

◆

She's always had vivid dreams, but this seems like an especially bad one. Yet no matter how she tries, she can't remember its details. All she knows is that it involved Nicky and that somehow he'd been terribly hurt or broken.

She walks out to the kitchen and pours a tiny glass of her special pick-me-up, Southern Comfort, then opens the window, leans out into the night and takes a deep breath. The cold air and the sharpness of the drink make her crave a cigarette.

As she cups the match inside her hand, she catches sight of her reflection in the other pane of glass. Somehow the light of the fire looks tangled in the mass of her hair, and the image it leaves in her mind is terrifying. How she could just ignite, go up in smoke like Joan of Arc. Spontaneously combust, leaving Nicky alone.

Sitting on the kitchen chair, she pulls hard on the cigarette to get the hot breath of the smoke into her lungs. She enjoys the sear of pain that fries on that pale skin down there. As if it were a cleansing, a punishment, a hurt.

When she finishes it, she lights another and then another

one off of that. By then the pale crack of sun has begun to creep its way along the sky. And she knows the night is almost over, so she makes her way back to bed.

Eight.

Reggie still thinks a lot about how great it would be if she and Nick could get a house. The notion of a yard and a dog seems like such a good dream. She doesn't like to mention it to Nicky, because she doesn't want to get his hopes and feelings up.

She remembers back when she'd been in Grade One how they'd been given oversized sheets of paper for an important art project. Each of them was supposed to draw a big picture of the people in their family standing beside the house where they lived. She hopes that maybe with the collapsing family, and people not living in houses so much anymore, schools are getting more merciful about asking for this sort of thing.

But just in case they aren't, she wants to be ready.

She knows that Nicky doesn't have much of a family to put into that kind of portrait. Maybe that's one of the reasons getting a dog seems so important. Probably even better than getting a brother would be. A brother would mean going through the whole baby thing again. And she knows she can't afford that, not in money or time or sanity.

But a house, now, that's something she might actually get. A house with a yard and a fence around the back. If she starts looking soon, she thinks, she might even be able to find them one before Nicky starts going to real school.

She remembers how much fun she and Brian used to have, how great so many of their days in his house had been. But she also recalls how hard it had been the year Brian went away to blind school. He didn't know how to write letters, so that had been that. But at least he'd come home for Christmas.

His return had made the holiday that much better for both of them. Presents were supposed to be important, but much more important was the privacy of their friendship and their fort time. Brian had told Reggie he was learning how to read, and showed her the bumps on the pages in his thick, white books. He'd let her feel the bumps, but she couldn't tell one from the other. He told her maybe blind kids get better fingertips than kids who can see.

Instead of trying to figure out the bumps, she'd offered to read to him from some of the books his parents had, the ones they used for weighing down the corners of the forts they built. There were lots of big, heavy thick ones, full of pictures that were outlined in fancy black swirls. Books filled with photos of people wrapped in bandages, or hung with slings, locked into contraptions. These were the books that so often distracted Reggie.

She'd found a great one, full of amputations and other medical wonders. And though she was mostly describing the pictures, and not really reading at all, Brian sat in silent awe, listening carefully to her voice.

"And in this one, there's a man with a little arm that ends just above his elbow, only there's a tiny, perfect set of fingers there. It looks like he's reaching out to shake your hand or something. *Ewwww.* I don't think I'd want to touch his hand, do you?"

"I don't know. I wonder what it'd feel like. What does it look like? Does it have fingernails?"

"I can't really see that close, but I told you, except for being so little, it looks like a regular hand. Only it *is* kind of sticking up funny, like it's bent or something."

"Maybe it's hard for the man to reach for things. Maybe he's had to try stretching it to make it work better."

"Maybe. I don't know."

Reggie kept turning the pages, and knew she had Brian hooked. He wanted to know about everything that was in the books. They'd spent the whole afternoon with her describing surgery scars, hernias, and various deformities of both accident and birth. When it was nearly dark, and time for her to go home, they'd agreed to continue the saga the following day.

◆

Only she also remembers another time, one of those following days. Since it was Christmas, Mr. MacKenzie showed up. He brought so many presents you might have thought he was Santa. He'd even brought a gift for Reggie and told her to open it right away. That had been something she wasn't sure about doing. At her house, nobody opened anything before Christmas morning, and even then not until the breakfast dishes had been washed and put away.

She'd stood there holding the parcel, looking hard at it, then moved her eyes up to Mr. MacKenzie's face, and back to the parcel again. He'd laughed in the big loud way he had, and told her she didn't have to open it if she didn't want to, but maybe, if she wasn't a good girl, it would disappear – fly right back to the North Pole where it had come from. And then he'd laughed some more, at something he must have said, and his wife had laughed right along with him. Mrs. MacKenzie looked glad that he was home, like she could have laughed at anything.

So Reggie hadn't waited, had ripped off the ribbon and paper. Brian had wanted to know right away, "What is it, what is it? Tell me, tell me."

It had been a fuzzy rabbit, with a key stuck into its back. She'd never heard of anyone getting a rabbit for Christmas.

She thought a rabbit was maybe something for Easter, but not for Christmas.

"Well," Mr. MacKenzie had asked, "aren't you going to wind him up, Reggie? See how he can hop? See how he hops after that carrot top of yours?"

And again, there'd been the burst of laughter, too loud and too long, with Mrs. MacKenzie joining in, breasts bouncing up and down, pulling at the stretched wool of her sweater. Only Brian, still not quite getting it. Only Brian, her ally against the noise of it all.

And she'd grabbed her coat and run out the door and hadn't come back until a few days later, after she was sure Mr. MacKenzie had gone away again.

Nine.

That afternoon Harmon comes by without warning. It's a Tuesday and Reggie has the day off. Apparently Harmon has time away from the store too.

Reggie's kept Nicky home with her that day, even though he isn't sick, even though she knows she should have taken him to his playschool group, that she'll have to pay the day's fee anyway. But it seems with every day closer he gets to real school, the more time she wants to spend with him.

She's in the kitchen cleaning up the few dishes from their lunch when a knock comes at the door. Nicky calls out, "I'll get it!" and opens, to be greeted by Harmon.

"Sorry for coming by like this. Without phoning and all," he apologizes, tilting his head, trying to see into the apartment past Nicky. "The door downstairs was open, so I let myself in."

"That's okay, Harmon," says Nicky. "Come on in."

As Reggie walks out to the living room, she's drying her hands on a tea towel. Harmon's still standing outside in the hallway, but clearly he's expecting that she's going to ask him in.

When she doesn't, he raises the question, "Aren't you going to ask me in?"

With the answer seeming so obvious, the directness of his words is enough to fluster her. This must show on her face, for he continues, "Unless, of course, you're busy. I know I should have called."

She opens the door the rest of the way and asks him to come in, apologizing for the mess all over the living room. She and Nicky have set up a road course on the floor, and the little metal cars are still scattered about from where they've been running their pretend races.

"Hey, I'm not complaining," and he gingerly steps around and through the maze of ropes and belts they've set out as guard rails for their track.

Nicky calls out, "Don't step on Michael Angretti!"

"Hey pal, I don't mean to step on anybody – especially if they might get mad."

The three of them make their way into the kitchen and Harmon sits down at the table. Reggie doesn't know if it's too early for beer, but she offers him one anyway while she cleans up the card game she'd had earlier with Nicky.

"No thanks, I'm driving," he says, nodding towards the little cars.

Reggie isn't quite sure if this is a serious 'no' or not. Whatever, she thinks, and turns to put the kettle on.

By this time, Nicky has climbed up into Harmon's lap. As he likes to do so often, he's fingering Harmon's ring. The ring is golden and formed in the shape of a skull. He's always told Nicky that it's his pirate ring, though Reggie knows better: it was Harmon's dad's, from when he'd been in the war. And she is pretty sure that he'd been a pilot, not a pirate.

The two males have bonded, or whatever the term is. She can see it in the way they both hold their heads at the same angle. One of those things involving certain breeds of dogs. You can tell when you've got their attention by the way they incline their head to some specific angle. One of those goofy studies – something or other like that. But then maybe males really are sort of like dogs: Keep them fed and patted up, and they stay loyal and happy.

The kettle starts to screech, and Nicky reaches to cover his ears. He's always done that. Maybe he really is part dog, with hearing that's more sensitive than regular people-hearing. "Coffee or tea, Harmon, you make the call."

"Coffee sounds great."

"Okay, but all I've got is instant."

"Not a problem. Most of the time, I'm pretty much an instant man."

She spoons the brown crystals into two cups, and follows this by pouring in the fresh boiling water. When she reaches into the fridge, she grabs the milk for creaming the coffees and a container of juice as well. Nicky seems happy with his glass of apple juice and drinks it down in nearly one gulp. Then he hops down from Harmon's lap and heads to the other room where he resumes his *vrooming* around their track.

"So, what brings you over here when you get the day off?"

Harmon seems to hesitate, as if he needs to think some more about what he means to say. She wonders if he's trying to tell her that they're breaking up. Only really, she wonders, what is there to break up from?

He reaches for her hand. She meets him with hers. His is super-warmed from holding the side of his cup. "Reggie," he says. "I've been thinking about us."

Uh-oh, she thinks, I was right. Amazing.

"Not just you and me either. You and me and Nickolas. I can't help but think that we make a fine team." He looks up from where he's been staring at the table. "Reggie, I guess I'm not very good at this, but I'm asking you to marry me."

Reggie figures it's a good thing that she's sitting down. This is just too out of the blue for words. She's never even slept with the man – for that matter, has barely kissed him. This is really crazy. Holy shit.

"I'm sorry if you think I'm being out of line." He's withdrawn his hand from where it had rested around hers and has wrapped it instead around the security of his coffee mug again. "I'm sorry for being so bold. I'll leave if you want me to," he says, putting down the cup and rising from the chair.

She stands up too, and reaches to touch his arm. "Oh, Harmon, it isn't that. You just took me by surprise. Y'know, it isn't every day a girl gets proposed to. Getting married really isn't a thing that's been on my mind."

"Are you two getting married, Mum?" Nicky has reappeared.

"Well, Jeez, Nick, I don't know," she says.

"Say yes, say yes, say yes!" he jumps up and down.

With a persuader like that, what is she supposed to say? She smiles and looks at Harmon and they hug – and that, it seems, is that.

◆

She lies awake in bed for a long time that night, wondering what she's gone and got herself into. For one thing, she is still alone in the bed. If they're really going to be married, sleeping alone seems awfully strange, but Harmon has insisted on this part. Claims it isn't proper yet. That they'll do things right. That this is a big chance for both of them to start over.

She has no idea if any of this is right. Though Nick sure seems to care for Harmon, and that in itself carries its own peculiar weight.

Is it fair to expect a boy to grow up without a father? Sure, things are easy enough while he's still little and sweet, but what about when he turns fourteen and decides to hate everyone? How easy will that be for her if she's still on her own?

She wishes she had a sister or some friend who was close. What with bad relationships of one sort and another, it seems she's burned a lot of bridges and turned into kind of a loner. And then, after she and Randy split and Nicky'd needed so much of her attention, work and a place to live had become about all she'd found time to deal with. Sure, there are some of the girls from the store. She's gone out with them from time to time, and even to a few parties at some of their houses, but the realization comes to her as she lies there looking at the ceiling: Except of course for Nicky, she really doesn't have a single friend.

Coupled with confusion over how she feels about the day's events, this understanding is just enough to put her over the top on the proverbial self-pity scale. Here she is, on the day she's been proposed to, supposedly one of the happiest days of her life, crying herself to sleep, soaking the pillow and her dreams.

◆

I am walking alone, and I can't see where I'm going. I can feel cobwebs – stringy bits everywhere – hanging down as if from the ceiling. I keep brushing into them, no matter which way I turn.

I have to keep my mouth closed tight so they don't go in. I know they will be bitter if I taste them, maybe even poisonous. They are dangerous and probably filled with armies of miniature spiders. One arm is in front of me, held out like a beacon, only my arm has such a tiny hand way out there at the end.

I convince myself the hand is small because I am holding it out so far, so very far in front of me, but I fail at this, I know better. It has shrunken to the size of a Barbie doll hand. Soon, if I don't get out of this place, the rest of me will shrink this way too. Only not all at once. Bit by bit, part by part. Wherever I touch the webs, I shrink. Shriveling, I gradually turn into tiny, useless pieces.

◆

She doesn't start work until eleven the next morning, which is a good thing, considering all she has to do to get her eyes to look normal again.

Harmon, on the other hand, has been in the store since before eight, and he hasn't wasted any time announcing their 'engagement'. Every time she hears the word, she can feel people gawking down at her hand, looking for a diamond. After a while, she notices that she's covering her left hand nearly every time someone else in the store comes up to offer congratulations.

Gloria shares the lunch room with her and does her best to pump Reggie for details. About their wedding, about their plans for the future, and most of all, about Harmon. Gloria's questions make Reggie realize just how little she knows about this man. This man she is supposedly going to marry. From this day forward, along with all the rest of it.

Reggie tells Gloria she's sorry, that she doesn't feel very sociable. Says she has a killer headache and that she needs a power nap. Could she maybe just let her have a lie-down, please. A quick little nap on the couch?

"Sure, honey. I understand. Big night last night, eh?" Gloria winks and heads for the exit. "I've got some paperwork I should catch up on anyway. Don't be too long now. Sweet dreams," she coos, and closes the door behind her.

Oh man, thinks Reggie, as she lights herself a smoke. Let's hope there's a power out and that the store closes early. This girl wants outta here and soon.

Ten.

The next couple of weeks are busy, as Harmon has found them a house. When he announces this, Reggie is more than a little surprised. Not that he's found a house, but that he's done so without consulting her.

When she tries to tell him that she feels left out by this, he just pats her shoulder and tells her she already does enough for this family. And, besides, she and Nicky are going to love the place. That they'll all go together and see it on the weekend.

◆

I am in the women's washroom of some fancy hotel. One of those places where there's an anteroom that looks like an old-fashioned parlour, but with fancy light fixtures and gilt-framed mirrors all around. It's separate from the other room that has the sinks and stalls. And who walks through the doorway but my Gramma. She is wearing the same rose-coloured suit she wore when she was laid out in her coffin.

Even though I see her standing there, I know that she is dead. I remember all the details: that I was nine when she had the heart attack – so unexpected – and that she was still in her fifties when it happened. Only now, here in this place, she must be at least ninety, she looks so old.

She wants to lie down, says that she feels tired. To not let her sleep too long, to please be sure to wake her. She doesn't want to miss out on the roast beef dinner. That she's heard there'll be gravy and Yorkshires.

"I will, I promise," I tell her. "I'll wake you up. I won't let you sleep through the food."

And she closes her eyes before I can say anything more, and promptly falls asleep.

But I want to tell her about Nicky and how big he is, how smart he is, how much he sometimes looks like Grampa. And then her mouth droops open, and I see the edge of her tongue nudging the side of her lips. A string of drool begins to form and glides down towards the line of her jaw. I reach to take a tissue from a box that is resting on one of the fancy mirror-topped tables. I see my face reflected there, and see that I am old too.

◆

The house isn't exactly what Reggie has imagined, but she has to admit, it isn't all that bad either. It's reasonably simple, with nothing too fussy, though it does have one of those overdone, fancy chandeliers in the dining room. Nicky of course loves this ridiculous touch, and keeps turning the fountain of lights on and off until she's afraid he'll wear out the dimmer switch.

But whether she likes it or not, it seems that the house is a done deal. Harmon has signed them on for a two-year lease. All that remains is for them to move in, and the end of the month is less than a week away.

"But I have to give my notice. I've been in the building too long to just walk away."

"Nothing to worry about. I talked to the manager already. Didn't want there to be anything to stand in our way."

This leaves Reggie feeling a little disconcerted, but she doesn't know exactly what to say, what in fact to complain about, so she decides to let it pass. She knows that he's only trying to make things easy for her.

The rest of the house is fine. As Harmon has announced, there is even a playroom. It's a funny kind of room, skinny and probably planned originally as storage, but Nicky marches right in and claims it. "I can be a pirate in here. There's even a spot for my spy glass."

Spy glass is what Nicky has taken to calling his telescope, a gift from Harmon for his fifth birthday last month.

Harmon is beaming. "Looks like that territory's been claimed."

There's a little round window at the back of the long room. Almost like a porthole out from the rear of the house. The yard has a few decent trees too, clumped together nicely for a woodsy effect.

When they walk around the yard, Reggie finds a spot where she thinks they could make a garden. "There'd be enough sun, and the hose hook-up is handy."

The only thing wrong with the yard is that it doesn't have much of a fence – just some falling down split rail, but Harmon says that they can fix that later. Besides, they don't need a fence right away. They don't really need to get a dog. After all, he kids, they've got him now, don't they.

They go back inside the house and walk around some more, and Reggie forces herself to try to be more agreeable. She talks about where she might put some of her things and how they might want to paint the kitchen a better colour. It's the one room that somehow looks dingy. It smells as if the last people who lived here must have cooked a lot of fried food. It holds a hangover atmosphere of nearly-rancid grease. Even the little garage looks better-kept.

The master bedroom is the room that Harmon has saved for last. The walls are a fresh pale blue and the closet is huge.

There is even an en-suite, complete with a big claw-foot tub. Reggie has to admit, as far as bedrooms go, this is spectacular. A bay window looks out toward the back, focusing on that copse of young trees she's noticed. From here she can also see just how close it is to the school. Why, you can practically look out onto the playground from in here.

At last she gives in, allows herself to be enthusiastic. "Oh, Harmon, I love it. It's perfect!" And she throws herself into his arms and relaxes her body against his, for maybe the very first time.

Eleven.

All things considered, the wedding isn't as bad as it might have been. Nobody, including Harmon, has expected very much. After all, it isn't as if it's the first time for either of them. Neither of them has any family around, so who do they need to impress?

Reggie has a hard time coming up with someone as her bridesmaid, but finally thinks to ask Tess, the older woman from down the hall in the building, the one who so often babysits Nicky. Tess has helped out a few times when Reggie's found herself in a bind because she's been called at the last minute to fill in for somebody's shift at the store. And here she is again, in kind of a pinch, so maybe it makes sense that Tess would be the one to ask.

As it turns out, Tess is thrilled by the request. She buys herself a new pink dress along with a jacket and shoes to match. When she confesses what she's paid to Reggie, she laughs and says that she hasn't spent that much on herself in years, but that it's an extravagance she enjoys.

Harmon has asked Stan, the assistant manager from the store, to stand up as his best man. Reggie thinks Stan looks surprisingly good in his dark blue pinstripe suit, a major shift from the generic red lab coat she's used to seeing him wear.

Quite a few of them from the store have shown up at the little reception they're having. In fact, if it weren't for Tess and Nicky and everyone's dress-up clothes, the party would seem almost like being at work.

The guests all seem to assume that between them, she and Harmon have all they need to set up house. So the gifts as such are really nothing special. In fact, most of them turn out to be home-tampered dirty-joke prizes – condoms with holes that have been paper-punched in them, things that make Reggie want to roll her eyes while she does her best to keep Nicky distracted. There are also bits of cash pinned onto the branches of a money tree. This turns out to be one idea which isn't really so bad, though it makes Reggie feel a bit as though they're someplace in 19th century Europe. She almost wants to check and see that they're dollars, not *kopeks* or *rubles* or something equally exotic and useless hanging by their safety pins, adorning the scrawny branches of the little tree.

Tess gives her a cookbook, though she apologizes for doing so, saying a modern young working girl probably doesn't have time for that sort of thing, *but*. She is also taking Nicky to stay at her place while Reggie and Harmon go on their overnight honeymoon. Just one night at a fancy hotel, but a night alone at least.

Gloria has organized the girls, got them all to pitch in, and then she's gone out and bought a lacy negligée set in a shockingly deep shade of purple. It's the last thing in the world that Reggie might have thought to ask for, but as things turn out, it seems to be exactly what Harmon would have wished her to get.

◆

After leaving the reception, the newlyweds drive Nicky and Tess back to the apartment building and say their good-byes, with big hugs all around. Reggie promises she'll call sometime the next morning, though not to expect it to be very early. She reminds Tess about where they're staying, but Tess only laughs and promises she'll remember, says she won't be bothering them and not to worry about a thing. That no five-year-old boy, especially one as sweet as Nicky, can present her with more than she can handle. "At least," she adds, "not in less than twenty-four hours."

Their reservations are for the hotel's bridal suite, and Reggie can't help but cringe over that. Here she has just finished dropping off her child, and twenty minutes later she's checking in to the fucking bridal suite. Although something in the back of her mind clicks at the thought of the fucking part. Yes, that is something she is ready for.

But first, Harmon explains, they have to go to dinner. He's made reservations at a restaurant just down the street. Stan has promised him, best prime rib in town.

Reggie doesn't feel much like eating prime rib, not after all the olive spread and bits of cake she's had at the reception. Though a bottle of thick red wine sounds tempting. And she does want her marriage to get off on the right foot.

So when Harmon holds out his arm for her, she takes the bait and rests her hand daintily just inside his elbow. And down the aisle of the narrow sidewalk they parade, man and wife.

◆

Reggie doesn't drink nearly as much as she used to. Because Harmon doesn't seem to consider booze an everyday thing, she finds she's out of the habit. So the red wine he's ordered has given her quite the buzz.

She hasn't been able to eat much, even though the meal is good, with the meat cooked exactly the way she likes it. Harmon doesn't complain though, calls it "Wedding Night Nerves," gazes knowingly into her eyes. She is feeling drunk enough that it is hard for her not to giggle at his expression.

When they get back to the room, she suggests they take a bath. He thinks it's fine if that's what she wants to do, but says he wants to see if there's anything on TV.

His not wanting to join her in the Jacuzzi leaves her a little disappointed, but oh well, she thinks, I'll just have to try to persuade him.

The oversized tub looks big enough to swim in. While it fills with hot water, she undresses down to panties and bra, then peels off the foil top from the complimentary bottle of champagne. While she twists at the wire cage on the cork, she does a kind of shimmy dance, shaking her ass in Harmon's direction, trying to tempt him to join her in the tub. He laughs at her and tells her to go ahead, explaining that he is already clean. To go ahead and enjoy herself, to relax. "Take yourself a deep one," he suggests to her. "We might as well get our money's worth out of this place."

Lying in the big tub, she looks up at the ceiling. There is actually a mirror up there. She thinks about how much fun this might have been. There's plenty of room for the two of them. She wonders, considering the set-up, if any other man she's ever been with would have been sitting in front of the television.

Somehow she doubts it. No, it's more than a shiver of doubt. And then it strikes her and grabs her: Harmon is gay. She and Nicky are merely props so he'll look hetero. What the hell has she gone and got herself into anyway?

◆

But no, her theory is wrong. Harmon isn't gay. Or, at least he doesn't seem to mind doing it with a woman. Turns out, he just isn't exactly a whole bunch of fun when it comes time for the sack.

She rationalizes the night's events, makes up excuses — maybe he was tired after all that had happened that day. And maybe the wine and champagne hadn't helped him any either. Still, she replays the whole crazy scene.

When Reggie'd come out of the bathroom, Harmon had been lying in the bed, sheets pulled up past his waist, looking like he was waiting for her, finally ready. The dark hair on his chest had looked wonderful to her and the thought of rubbing her breasts in it had nearly made her ache.

She could tell he loved how she looked in the new negligée. She'd seen the look on his face when she'd opened the box at the reception, and had been glad she'd had the sense to put it on for him, even though it had seemed kind of ridiculous to be wearing anything at all. She'd had to admit, though, the deep purple colour did make a nice complement to her hair and made her skin look creamy and delicious. Still, she'd noticed the way the fabric had felt itchy when she'd pulled it over her head. Something about the way the lace was attached made it sharp and scratchy at the edges.

And when she'd lifted off the frothy gown, turning slowly for him to admire her, he'd looked like he might have been blushing, seemed surprised by the orange of her bush. "What did you expect," she'd asked, "that it'd be blonde?"

He'd seemed flustered by the bluntness of her question, said something about not ever thinking about how she'd look 'down there'. And with that he'd pulled her under sheets, shoved himself into her and come.

◆

Okay, she keeps trying to tell herself. Maybe it hadn't been as bad as all that. But it had been kind of a quickie, that was for sure. And he had been wearing a condom. But maybe that was just good sense, as they'd never talked about birth control. Though he'd also got up and done what sounded like a heck of a lot of washing in the bathroom afterwards.

The last thought Reggie has before joining Harmon in their first sleep together is that things can only get better.

◆

Nicky is playing pirates in his long skinny playroom. Only the room is somehow much more like the inside of a school bus. There are straight-backed seats arranged in crazy patterns. They don't go side-by-side and back-to-front in rows. They are arranged helter-skelter, going in all different directions. Who could know which way is supposed to be the front?

And who but Brian MacKenzie crawls out from under a row of seats. He is on his hands and knees and looks to be the same age he used to be so long ago, just about the same age as Nicky is now. Nicky acts aloof and seems to ignore or maybe not see him. Brian scoots across the aisle like an oversized beetle and darts back to hide under some seats. He emerges now and then from unexpected places. This is supposed to be some kind of a game that he has invented. He was always so good at navigating under things, as if he had some kind of built-in radar – maybe because he was blind. Never got bruises on his forehead, never needed bangs to cover the purple marks.

I realize how much I miss Brian, his unconditional friendship. He never cared what I looked like, never even knew about my stupid orange hair.

I reach for Brian, wanting to hold him, but he is as evasive as a pinball, the way he manoeuvres back and forth beneath the scattered benches. And the dream fades into greyness, but not before I realize that what I'm looking at – no, more a looking into – is a glimpse, I think, allowing me to see the grey that Brian sees.

Twelve.

Christmas comes fast, or maybe it just seems that way. Whatever it is, Reggie keeps thinking she doesn't feel quite ready.

She has done more than she usually does preparing for the holiday. Somehow this has come to seem necessary to her now that they all live in a house and are trying hard to be more of a real family.

Nicky wants so badly to help with the baking, but Reggie gets discouraged by the messes he makes. In the end, she does most of it after he's gone to sleep, going to bed herself much closer to midnight – some nights, even later.

She finds that, more and more often, she is going to bed later than Harmon. In a way, this makes sense, as he almost always has to be at the store by seven or even earlier, where her shifts never start before half past nine or ten. Besides, she has to face it, their sex life isn't exactly the greatest, so what's the point in trying to get to bed the same time he does?

It isn't that the sex is terrible. It's okay, but awfully predictable. She supposes they still do it reasonably often. Often at least as the average one-point-whatever-it-is times a week. It's just that, when it happens, she doesn't exactly hear bells. While the habit of condoms hasn't helped in the turn-on department, it has allowed Reggie to quit taking her pills. They'd always made her feel bloatish and squishy, and really, she figures, why bother. She can't imagine he's got a single active sperm inside him.

Stranger yet is his practice of after-washing, a routine that hasn't eased much, and is hardly inspiring. She's thought more than once, that for all his good looks, he simply isn't very sexy. Figures maybe all of his hormones are wasted, too busy pumping up that thick head of wavy dark hair.

Once, in the middle of it, if you could call any of it the middle – it usually seems to be over before it's barely started – she'd caught herself having to choke down a laugh. She'd remembered something Harmon had said to her about being an instant kind of guy. He hadn't been kidding about that. Too bad she hadn't realized then that he didn't only mean coffee.

Besides getting used to quickies – ones that are nearly always protected – she is getting used to him. And though she can't pretend he sets her heart in rapid-fire motion, she has certainly developed more than a fondness for him. She's been trying so hard with this perfect wife thing, she is actually knitting him a sweater.

She thinks about how she'd fooled around with crafts when she'd been a kid, stringing beads or knitting endless multi-coloured scarves. Looking back, she realizes that those creative urges might have been part of the reason she'd enjoyed Home Ec in high school. At least the sewing part of that class had given her a few good memories. And there was something satisfying about making your own clothes. Something sort of homesteady, a back-to-the-hearth kind of thing.

She's had trouble keeping the project hidden and out of the way, and has been careful not to work on it except when she's alone, with Nicky gone to school and Harmon off at work. She knows it's probably silly not to bring it out when only Nick is around, but she does so want it to be a surprise, and she still isn't sure whether he'll be able to keep such a big secret. But now that the day is getting so close she's been regretting this decision, and finds herself having to sneak in her quota of rows after both of the guys have gone to sleep, leaving her to the quiet of late night in the house.

It hasn't turned out to be a bad house after all, even though she still isn't wild about the gaudy-looking chandelier. Nicky remains enchanted by it, and even Harm has tried to convince her how good it will look shining down on their Christmas dinner.

Yes, she has at least convinced him to let her abbreviate his name. She feels more comfortable calling him Harm. It seems less offensive to her ear, and he's finally gotten used to her calling him that.

Nicky still calls him Harmon, though Harm wishes he'd call him Dad. Nicky doesn't seem to see the importance of this, as he has, after all, first come to know him by his given name. It's what he's used to, that's all, no offence meant. And Harm seems to take it pretty well in stride.

He also seems to be getting excited about what he calls the Big Surprise, the Christmas gift he's buying for the whole family. Reggie tries hard not to get her hopes too high, but she has her fingers crossed for a dishwasher, even a used one. She still doesn't understand how a house pretentious enough to have a chandelier could be without a dishwasher.

Oh well, designed by a man, she thinks to herself. What can you expect?

And finishes off another row and packs the growing sweater back into its cubby on her side of the closet.

◆

As she's getting out of the bathtub, she catches a glimpse of herself in the mirror. It makes her do a double-take. That can't be her.

She finishes rubbing herself with the towel and looks at her body again. Jesus, she's getting thick at the middle. She looks like a fucking pig.

Because her old scale is the wrong colour for the room, she keeps it stashed away in the cupboard under the bathroom sink. It's heavy, and awkward to dislodge, but she persists and drags it out of its place. She sets it on the floor and steps on it.

Shedding the towel she has wrapped around her wet hair doesn't make even a pound of difference. This is disgusting. She is sure she isn't pregnant. She'd had her period – when exactly – three weeks ago? Had it been more? How can she weigh this much? What the hell has happened to her? Has getting married done something to her, has it made her think she can just let herself go?

When she tries pushing the scale back into the cupboard, she manages to scratch a gouge into the finish on the inside of the door. With another heave she shoves it back into the dark where it belongs. Not only is she getting fat, she's starting to think in terms of all those stupid magazines. The ones she has to look at every day beside her check-stand. The ones she has to restock, it seems, continuously. The ones that tell their readers how to keep their hubbies happy. Are their stories that contagious? Can their inanities be getting to her? Is she really turning into the Fat Canadian Housewife?

She gets into her uniform, makes herself an egg and toast. Then she throws the food away and marches out the door.

◆

She is looking at the ceiling. Bright lights are shining into her eyes. She thinks for a minute she must be in a delivery room, having another baby.

And then there is Harmon, looking down into her face. Not a nurse named Paula or whatever it had been when Nicky'd been born.

"Reggie, are you all right?" He is sort of shaking her.

"Ummm. What happened?"

"They think you fainted, Reg, only you wouldn't wake up. They paged me over from produce and I got here fast as I could. You gonna be okay now, baby?"

She likes it when he talks to her with fuzzy names. It makes her feel all sexy, like maybe one day he might still turn into some kind of super stud.

She notices other faces now. She has earned herself a crowd. Harmon helps her up to her feet and sets her in a chair that someone has brought. Gloria tells her she better go home until she is feeling better. Besides, that's a nasty bruise starting to swell up on the side of her face. Reggie reaches to touch the spot on her cheek where it hurts the most. She must have banged it good on something, it's already puffy-feeling.

Harmon says he'll go and get her jacket so he can take her home. It's nearly his lunch break so he says that it isn't any trouble. It seems to take him only a second to fetch her coat. Maybe someone else has already figured out that she'll be needing it and has brought it from the lunch room – has it waiting, arms ready, like a fireman's coat.

Reggie feels out of it as he wraps the jacket around her, but she isn't out of it enough not to notice the little fist and thumb Gloria raises toward Harmon. Reggie recognizes immediately what she is signalling him, "Way to go there, Pops. Congratulations!"

Realizing what they think, Reggie nearly faints again, but she knows it isn't the time to make a protest. Just smiles wanly at the crowd and twiddles her fingers like the queen and lets Harmon guide her out of there to the waiting car.

◆

Harm brings in a tray and feeds her tomato soup and crackers while she lies propped up in the bed. She tells him he's overdoing it, that there's nothing wrong with her. At the most, maybe a touch of flu, after all, 'tis the season.

"Never mind. Just eat this up and take a little nap." She can hardly eat the soup, he's perched so close to her – jiggling the bed so much she can hardly balance the bowl. Jesus Christ, he must think that Gloria is right. Oh well, she'll be getting her period any day this week now. She'll be sure to let him know as soon as it shows up.

He tucks her in and asks if she wants anything else. Says he'll take the tray back into the kitchen. She has to admit, the bed feels good. And the painkiller he's given her is starting to kick in, so maybe a bit of rest won't be so bad after all.

She's just about asleep, not even sure if it's some kind of dream, but she thinks she hears him humming, like he's practising a lullaby, "Away in a Manger." Fucking goddamn manger, no way.

Thirteen.

Christmas is spectacular, even though Santa hasn't brought Reggie her dishwasher. The Big Surprise turns out instead to be a state of the art camcorder. "It could have been worse," she has explained to Tess, "it might have been a table saw."

Reggie has invited Tess to join them for the dinner, and has got up early, stuffed the turkey and even made a pumpkin pie. Now that they've eaten the meal, she's feeling sleepy. She's heard that turkey has some sleep-inducing chemical in it. It's something natural in the meat, she's pretty sure, but just the same, it sounds creepy, drowsing out millions of people every Christmas and Thanksgiving.

When Harm volunteers to drive Tess back to her apartment, Reggie doesn't protest, says she'll do some cleaning up instead. And Tess doesn't object when Reggie offers to make her a package of leftovers. She puts in some big chunks of turkey meat and stuffing, along with a slice of the pie. She thanks Tess for bringing the lovely jellied salad, remarking on the appropriateness of the red and green theme, though she knows she'll probably dump the rest of it after Tess leaves.

Nicky even hugs Tess without having to be asked, which clearly makes her happy. Reggie thinks she sees a tear in Tess's eye.

Reggie and Nicky wave good-bye from the front window while Harmon backs the car out the driveway. It had meant a lot of work, but Christmas is worth it.

"How's about a nap there, Boy-O? We haven't had ourselves a super snuggle for too long a time."

Amazingly, despite the mountain of new toys, Nicky agrees and follows her down the hall to the big bedroom.

◆

The room is dim when Reggie wakes up, but it is a noise that wakes her. A whirring kind of funny sound. What the hell. "Who's there?" she calls, reaching for and finding the lamp switch.

Harmon is what's there, perched above the two of them. Standing on a goddamn ladder in the middle of the bedroom. Holding the fucking camcorder in front of his chest.

"I – I was just recording you. The two of you looked so peaceful. I just wanted to see how it worked."

Reggie brushes her hair away, out of her face where it's fallen. Reaches to push the covers back and realizes they are already down. As she gets out of bed and starts to head for the bathroom, she looks at him and shouts, "You know, you just about scared the living shit right out of me!" And again, as she decides instead to take Nicky to his room, "Don't ever pull a brilliant stunt like that again. Got that, Mr. Harmon. Understand?"

And she lifts up her son, even though he is much too heavy, and cradles his head in her hand as they leave the silent room.

◆

I am holding a letter that has come as a surprise, mixed into the usual batch of assorted junk mail. The handwriting on the envelope is oddly familiar, though I can't immediately place who it belongs to. I admire its style though and stand the envelope against a wine glass, so that I can take my time and have a better look at it.

In the meantime the phone rings and I answer it without seeming to have to lift a receiver. A telephone has appeared here in the middle of the dining room table. It is not shaped like a phone though, but more like a turkey.

It is Harmon on the line, and he wants to know when I am going to come to bed. Says he got us the honeymoon suite and that the bath is getting cold. To speak up though, please, that he can hardly hear me – the jets of the Jacuzzi are making too much noise. This seems like a bad joke, and I manage to hang up on him, banging the telephone down somehow, even though I haven't actually been holding any receiver.

I smile and pick up a butter knife and slit open the letter. It looks even more appealing than it had before.

It turns out to be an invitation from Randy. Only he is now calling himself Randall, Lord of the Arts. I am so amazed by this I don't know what to do. I stuff the letter into its envelope and shove it into my bra.

◆

Harmon wants to pretend that nothing has happened. Says it's no big deal and that's supposed to be that.

But Reggie doesn't like it, though she can't say exactly why. She and Nicky were, after all, only sleeping, but something about the whole scene just doesn't feel right.

Nicky doesn't seem to remember that anything has happened. The old turkey sleeping pill must have really knocked him out. While she hasn't done too much to pry open his brain, she's made a few references to Harmon and his camera, but nothing seems to twig from him, nothing she can notice. He'll be going back to school in just a couple of days.

And although it's probably a bad time, money-wise and all, she is glad she's asked for some extra days off.

Even though she probably could have managed to arrange her days so Harm could be home some of the time she had to work, she's relieved at the thought that for one Christmas holiday Nicky doesn't have to go to a sitter at all.

It seems so much like old times, just the two of them. Only now they have a whole house to play in together.

One morning she wakes up early, as Harmon is getting ready to head out for work. It must have been the scraping sound of the shovel against the driveway that has pulled her out of this wintry morning sleep. Before Harm has finished shovelling, while the sun is still coming up, she and Nicky are bundling up to play in the newly fallen snow. By the time Harm is leaving for work, she and Nicky are packing snowballs and throwing them at his car as he backs out and drives away.

After breakfast they go outside again and build a sort of fort. When Nicky wants to come in to go to the bathroom, Reggie comes in too and makes them a Thermos of hot chocolate. When they go back out, the two of them sit down on the pair of snow thrones they've built. They sit there drinking hot milk behind the low walls of the fort, toasting each other with plastic cups, shouting *Skoal!* and *Cheers!* to each other. They stay outside even when the sun moves high in the sky and starts turning the fort into water. This is champagne, she thinks, this is the best. Truly the finest of wines.

Fourteen.

Valentine's is coming up, and Reggie's decided to try something romantic with Harmon for a change. Even though it falls on a Thursday, she knows the restaurants will be impossible. But for what she has in mind, that's just fine. And since the next day is going to be one of those province-wide teacher conferences, she's already asked Tess if she'll take Nicky for an overnight. In Reggie's mind Tess has become a kind of surrogate granny. She would never have the nerve to say this to Tess's face, because for all she knows, Tess might not be all that much older than Harmon. She's hard to place that way, sort of in-between age-wise.

Whatever, she sounds happy to take Nicky for the night. Even asks about videos he's allowed to watch, as she thinks that getting a movie might be fun for both of them.

Reggie waits for Thursday morning before telling Nick. Because she's wanted the plan to be a surprise for Harm, she's kept it from Nicky too. But she also wants to give him a bit of time to think about it, in case he doesn't feel comfortable staying away overnight again, so she tells him while he's eating his cereal. He seems excited though, and happy with the whole idea, especially when she tells him Tess is going to rent them a video. He wonders whether Tess will get *Death Race 2000*, a title she knows he's been eyeing for the checkered flags on its jacket. "No, Nicky, I don't think so. She's like me – she doesn't enjoy violence."

"What's violets?" he asks.

"Violence is when people hurt each other. But I know Tess will find something that's lots of fun to watch – and I bet she'll have something yummy for snack too." She feels a little guilty getting him so hyper before he goes off to school, but figures that with the Valentine's party they're having at the kindergarten, the teacher will have probably already braced herself for a wilder than usual kind of day. No wonder the teachers voted themselves a round of workshops for the following day.

◆

After Reggie drops Nicky at Tess's place, she goes home and finishes the preparations she'd started earlier. She's glad that this is one of those days she used to complain about, with less than a full shift at the store. Besides, with all the schools closed Friday, this translates as one of the best times for the teenagers who work there – they'll be available for a long weekend. And since they get paid less than she does with her seniority – well, she knows it all comes down to the old bottom line.

The dinner is going to be simple: steak and baked potato, with tinned corn and a bowl of lettuce salad. Nothing very fancy, that's how Harmon likes things. She has asked one of the guys in the meat department to get her some filet mignon, and he hands her the packet of freshly wrapped meat just as she's ending her shift. "Valentine treats, eh," he says, less of a question than a comment.

"Don't tell Harm though. It's a surprise."

"This is for *Harmon?*" he kids her. "Here I thought you were gonna ask *me* over, Reggie."

"Not this time, Vic," she laughs. "Gotta take a number with the rest of the guys. Just like in the bakery – fresh buns, y'know."

She leaves the store, smiling inside, glad she works in a place that can still be fun. Not one of those anal politically-correct offices she keeps reading about in the paper. What's the point, she thinks, if you can't even have a laugh?

◆

She knows Harm will be tired when he gets home from work, so she tells him to go have a lie-down on the couch. She offers to rub his back, but he says he's too exhausted for even that.

While she's getting dressed for dinner, she realizes how quiet the house is for this time of evening, and wonders how things might have been different if it had always been just the two of them, right from the start. If they'd met under different circumstances, at a different time.

There isn't really anything else left to do in the kitchen, as everything is ready as it can be. She's even opened the wine so it can breathe.

She hasn't done a crossword puzzle for a long while. Hasn't had the time, or maybe, she realizes, she must have given them up the same time she quit smoking. It's already been more than six months.

The new paint in the kitchen has probably helped motivate her out of that long-time habit. Though there are still times, even at her till, when a customer will come through, smelling of tobacco. She can sometimes feel herself wanting to ask them for a smoke, can picture herself standing outside in the parking lot with them, a sense of that old camaraderie. The getting-away-with-something feeling she'd had when she'd first started cigarettes. It's probably helped too that they can't smoke inside the lunch room any more. They're supposed to stand out back now by the big garbage bins, but everybody knows that Sylvia still smokes in the washroom. Knows it and lets her, but then she's maybe earned it. Besides, she'll be retiring before all that long. What the hell.

The puzzle is harder than Reggie remembers them being, but she supposes, like anything else, you lose a skill if you don't practise it. She has only about half the squares filled in, but she hears Harmon starting to stir, so she folds it over and tucks the paper away. Thinking of her plan for the evening, she hopes you don't have to lose all of your skills just because you don't practise them much.

◆

The dinner is fine, and Harmon seems happy, though he must have apologized twenty-five times over the fact that he hasn't done anything for her. That he hasn't realized what a romantic she is.

And with her sitting there in a satin dressing gown with jewellery on, really. How she looks like a queen all dressed up in red, that he hasn't realized Valentine's Day could be like a party.

She stands up, reaches out her hand, and puts it over his mouth, telling him to hush. "Ready for dessert yet?" she rubs her breasts against his head.

He clears his throat a bit but manages a little laugh. "Uh. I don't know. What's it going to be?"

"Coffee, tea or me?" she purrs. "Or better, how about you?"

He doesn't seem to understand what she means. She starts miming that she is undoing some buttons down the front of the robe, swaying a little in front of him while she does this, as if to sultry music. She turns away so he will get the full effect of what comes next, letting the gown do a slow glide down her back before she drops it to the floor. Turning around, she is holding her breasts, cupping the red brassiere in her hands. When she goes to bend towards him, she moves her hands away, revealing the hearts she's cut away for her nipples.

Harmon looks too surprised to say anything as she eases her g-stringed ass down on to his lap and rubs her now-hard nipples across his face. "What do you think, Harm. How 'bout a taste?" and she navigates her breast into his open mouth and pushes.

◆

Later, in the bathroom, Reggie wonders what she'd done wrong. She still had a mark across her stomach from where the thong's elastic had been. Okay, she was a little fat, probably too fat for such a get-up, but Jesus, she'd wanted to turn him on, make him really want her, just for once.

She thinks about the fiasco of trying to suck him. How at first she'd thought he was getting into the idea of sex play, and that pushing her head away was just a part of how he wanted it. But when he'd told her to quit, that what she was doing was filthy, and had he married himself a prostitute – well, Reggie'd got the message.

Harmon isn't normal, she thinks, sitting on the toilet. She's never before heard of a man who'd turn down a blow job. She's heard other women grumble about how their husbands or boyfriends are always begging them to go down on them, and that it isn't their favourite thing, but Reggie's always liked it. Likes the way men smell, slightly metallic, different than women. She knows this difference, its tangy salt taste – has licked her own fingers, likes that too.

She remembers that she hadn't liked it much when she'd been forced. Randy was always the worst for forcing. Loved to come home drunk at night, wake her up and shove it at her. Sometimes when she'd gag he'd get mad at her, hit her. No one would like that part though, would they.

She wipes, then flushes the toilet, turning to the sink. Looking in the mirror there, she doesn't like her face. She looks really tired, she thinks, maybe tired of trying. Splashing water over her eyes might help a bit. She has promised Nicky she will pick him up in the morning by nine, and she still has to clean up the kitchen, hide the foolish red clothes.

Later, when she finally crawls into bed, she nearly bursts out laughing, considering the sheer absurdity of this man lying there beside her, her lawful wedded husband. Or, as she thinks she remembers hearing, "Do you take this man to be your awful wedded husband?" That must have been what the man had said, all right.

Harmon, Mr. Not-So Normal, the man who says no to blow jobs, the man who likes to keep his little weenie safe and dry.

She thinks she should maybe phone the folks at the Guinness record books and report him.

And on the brink of sleep she wonders, do they pay?

Fifteen.

Winter slushes its way into early spring with barely any difference. The days are filled with heavy grey rains. Or at least that's the way it seems, not much light on the horizon.

Reggie and Nicky still hope for a dog, but Harmon says that with the new truck, there isn't any money for a fence. Besides he doesn't want one. So that, it seems, is that.

As a kind of compromise, Reggie buys a pair of goldfish. They're easy, just a bowl, some gravel and a jar of food. Nicky really likes them and even learns to change their water. Small responsibilities seem to suit him, satisfy him. She is glad to see that in him, wishes she'd had more of that. Someone who would maybe have expected more from her.

Nicky figures out names for them, Mr. Smart and Mr. Dumb. Reggie feels like Mrs. Dumb because she can't tell them apart. Nicky knows the difference – or claims he does – and tries to show her what it seems that only he can see.

Mr. Smart is alert to the world beyond the confines of the bowl, seems to watch for when the bright container of food comes out. Mr. Dumb never seems to notice Nicky standing there. Will only eat when flakes come by, floating into his face.

Mr. Dumb is not so dumb though, Reggie has to think. Only a few weeks later, it is Mr. Smart who shows up floating in the bowl.

◆

Shortly after Christmas, Harmon had convinced her that a truck would serve them better than the two small cars they had, especially where hers was needing work so often these days. As with most of their decisions, he seemed to have made up his mind before he'd presented the idea to Reggie, so she knew there wasn't much sense in trying to argue about it. Besides, she had to admit, the bus stop was really close and car repairs had been eating up a lot of her cheques lately.

The truck is one of those extra-longs, with a small back seat and a camper canopy. Although why they need all of that when they've never gone camping, she doesn't know. It keeps Harmon busy though, and Nicky likes to help him with the "fixing things up" – building the little room, complete with its bed and counter-top and safety-latching cupboards.

When they get the camper finished, Reggie is impressed. It comes as a surprise to learn that Harm is so handy. Funny thing. It makes her feel ashamed that she's never finished knitting his sweater. Here he's gone and started this project and seen it to completion in only a few weeks. She feels like a fraud and nearly tells him.

All the while the boys and their "fixing up" have been going on, the three of them have talked about a weekend trip of camping and fishing or hiking, but it never seems to happen. Harmon either has some job that needs doing around the house, or something will come up where he can't leave work. After all, he's now the assistant manager. Stan has moved, been transferred to another, bigger store.

That's why it is such a surprise when Reggie comes back from work one Friday night to find not only the truck gone, but Harmon and Nicky too. She had been thinking, as she'd walked home from the bus, how she would make a bowl of popcorn and see if they wanted to watch some junky movie on TV. Instead she finds a note on the kitchen table.

Dear Reggie,
Thought the weather seemed decent enough
to try out the camper. The boy and I
are off for a little fishing trip.
Will try to be back by Sunday afternoon.
Love,
Harmon

Well, that's a surprise. Nothing to indicate where they're going or whether they're going with anyone else. She wonders, does Harmon even have fishing gear around? She can't remember seeing any, but figures maybe he's borrowed some.

Oh well, she thinks to herself, popcorn still sounds fine.

◆

I am in a theatre, a fancy old vaudeville kind of place. Lots of ornate carvings, chandeliers and private boxes. In fact, I am sitting in one of those little rooms, perched above the stage by maybe twenty feet. Best seat in the house, I think. Let the show begin.

And miraculously, by magic, it does.

Thick velvet curtains rise, parting in the middle, lifting up in curves, the heavy folds of the drapes a harmonious symmetry.

A chorus line of dancers files in from the wings – patterns of swirling colour, a twirling synchronicity. A bubble of light, like a disco ball, floats down, barely touches the centre of the stage. Someone is in there, ready to step out. Maybe it is Glinda, Good Witch of the North.

But no, it is that little girl who used to come to the store, the one who wanted to buy her mother the cigarettes. In fact, she is smoking a cigarette herself, balancing it in one of those ridiculously long holders. She looks really silly, striding in circles around the stage, a little girl with make-up on, dressed in a frilly gown. She looks up and sees me, locks her big eyes into mine, tosses the cigarette and holder behind her. Turns her head in profile, faces me with her body, drops the gown from her shoulders and steps out of it in a single smooth move.

Standing there, she turns again, staring into my face, daring me to look at her, take pleasure in the sight of her. Little girl with dots for breasts, white-skinned pubic bone. One hand on her hip, she blows me a flirty kiss.

◆

Although she knows it has only been a dream, Reggie wakes in a tangle of sweat, feels upset and confused. Wonders what the hell is wrong with her anyway. Even though it's morning, she digs around in the back of a cupboard, covers the bottom of a mug with an inch of Southern Comfort.

Figures she is going nuts. Maybe needs a cigarette. Maybe needs a fuck is probably more like it.

Goes to take a shower, but phones the hair place first. Good chance for a cut today. No one around to do things for. Gets herself an appointment for the tail end of the afternoon. Finds herself a crossword and pours another drink.

◆

Why, she wonders, does it always feel so great when somebody else washes your hair? She loves the coconutty smell of the shampoo and the way the stylist doesn't seem afraid to really rub. This is so great, she thinks, trying to remind herself to do this more often.

Even though she hasn't been able to get in with her regular girl, she feels comfortable enough with the person they've given her instead. It's a guy for a change and he's actually pretty cute, cute enough she doesn't protest when he suggests she tries something different. Shorter, he thinks. Fluffier on top. Maybe even a little bit spiky. He demonstrates, holding the comb just so. He has won her over.

And it doesn't hurt that he loves her colour, jealous to hear that it's natural. "Come on. Does that mean that the other place...?" And he cuts off his thought mid-sentence, rolling his eyes towards the ceiling before he looks at her again, both of their faces in the mirror, snickering deliciously like a couple of teenagers.

He makes her feel comfortable and he makes it easy to laugh. She's almost a tiny bit sad that he is so obviously gay. He would probably appreciate getting his little dick sucked.

In fact, maybe it isn't so little, she thinks, just because he's skinny. Maybe he's got a big thick son-of-a-knackwurst in there, lurking inside the fly of his tight black pants.

Yeah, and maybe she's getting just too fucking horny. Maybe with nobody home and the new hairdo and all, maybe she ought to go out to the pub and see if she still knows how to get laid.

◆

Bad idea.

Late at night. She is in a dimly lit room that smells funny. Or maybe the funny smell is just her.

Bed springs squeak in protest as she rolls over. Sure enough, there is a man lying beside her. His bicep is practically in her face. A coiled rattlesnake is staring into her eyes. Luckily she doesn't scream when she sees the tattoo. As for the man, he is sleeping. She watches the rattler, moving up and down, rhythmically, in keeping with his quiet snores.

Unfortunately for her, she remembers more than she wants to, even this snoring man's name, Stu. Stu Martel.

She remembers and feels some sense of relief, that at least she'd had the sense to lie to him about her name. Told him it was Lucy. He'd laughed at that, but she didn't really think he'd got it, wasn't sure he knew the famous orange-haired Lucy.

That was all right, though. She hadn't picked him up for his brains. But hey, for a guy who claimed to be just passing through town, he sure could screw. In the sack at least, he seemed to know exactly where he was.

She could get wet again just thinking about it. How he'd sucked her and fucked her 'til she'd wanted to scream. And how he hadn't made a peep of complaint when she'd taken him in her mouth. How he'd let her suck him hard. How, when he'd come in her mouth, she'd swallowed it, smiling. And how he'd been ready again in almost no time at all.

She starts to turn to get out of the bed, but doesn't feel so shit hot when she tries to stand up. Must have been the cigarettes. What a stupid thing to do. Quit for half a year, then buy a pack and smoke nearly all of it. No wonder she feels so bad. No wonder her mouth tastes like somebody's old shoes.

She remembers that there's a bathroom across the way someplace and fumbles in the half-dark of the unfamiliar hallway, trying to find it without waking him. Fortunately for everyone, she finds it when she does, because as soon as she gets in there, her stomach turns inside out.

◆

It is still dark out when Reggie gets home. She'd tried to clean herself up, but knows she didn't do very well. Even the cab driver had made a sour face at her. She is just grateful now for her own bath and bed.

Lying in the tub, she feels like she is spinning, as if the water were encircling her in some kind of rotating cocoon. But she reminds herself that if it were, the water would be spilling out. Even if she felt like shit, it was good to know that gravity still ruled.

Drying herself with the towel, she looks into the mirror. Maybe she wasn't fresh out of the showroom anymore, but it was reassuring to know the old motor still worked.

Warm in flannel pyjamas, she settles her head on the pillow, giving in to its softness, grateful to be where she is. She knows it will be a while before she forgets what she's tasted tonight. And though she isn't too proud of her methods, she's glad she's gone and got herself tasted too. In fact, that part of the night had been something new for her. He'd turned her on her side and scissored her legs apart. Then he'd shown her how he liked going back and forth, up and down along her – eating, as he called it, corn on the bone.

◆

Reggie doesn't wake up until almost noon. She is surprised to find no one in the bed with her. But then all of it comes back, including the fact that Harmon has said they'll be home on Sunday afternoon. It must be getting close to that, so she knows she better get dressed.

She starts a load of wash, being sure to get all of her smoky things from last night in first, in case Nicky and Harmon show up early. She puts the sheets in too, in case she has carried any smells – of Stu or of the cigarettes – into the bed with her.

She knows she's done a stupid thing. What, in fact, if he had a disease? They had done everything any two people could do – or at least anything they could do that didn't hurt – that she could think of.

She makes up her mind that everything will be okay, even though she's well aware she's being naïve. Still, it's too late to do anything about it. And although the thought seems rotten, it almost makes her smirk to consider that, if she does have something now, Harm might get it too. Of course, it would have to be one of his rare, non-condomized nights. Still. Perfect Harmon the Puritan. Wouldn't that be something.

In between the folding and other cleaning up, Reggie thaws a chicken and puts it in the oven.

It is nearly eight when the guys finally get back. She thinks Nicky looks awfully tired, puffy little circles hanging grey beneath his eyes.

Harmon tells her not to worry, that both of them have eaten. That he will put the boy to bed, not to fuss.

She feels disappointed. Partly that they've eaten, that she isn't needed. Mostly though that Nicky hasn't seemed more glad to see her.

She goes to his room to tuck him in, but he's already asleep.

She goes back to the kitchen and eats both legs from the chicken before putting the rest of it into the fridge.

Harm comes out, still damp-looking, freshly shaved and showered. Tells her that he's going to bed, that he has an early day ahead.

Reggie puts her head back down to try to finish the weekend puzzle, the one she'd started yesterday, before she'd got her hair done. Finally sees an answer to a clue that had stumped her earlier. Thirty-seven down: *Not quite Marianne.* 'Unfaithful'.

Sixteen.

At supper that Monday night, Nicky makes an announcement. "Mr. Dumb is lonesome living by himself. Let's get him some friends he can play with while I go to school."

This makes sense to Reggie and she promises him they will. In fact, she tells him, "There's a pet shop really close to my bus stop by the store. Why don't I get him some little pals on my way home tomorrow?"

Nicky seems happy with this, and tells her he won't mind if she picks them out for him. That she can probably tell the kind of friends Mr. Dumb would like. With important matters settled, Nicky finishes his dinner and asks to be excused.

When Nick has gone to his room, Reggie asks Harmon how the fishing had been. Had they caught anything?

He is fooling around with the peas on his plate, swirling them around with his fork in the gravy, mushing them into the potatoes. "Oh, it was fine," he says, sounding noncommittal. "Fish weren't really biting though. We mostly did a little exploring. Guess it was more just the getaway I needed."

"I know what you mean," she says. "I got my hair cut while you were away. D'you like it?"

Finally, he lifts his eyes toward her, looking up from where he's been playing with his food. "Sorry. I didn't notice. You know I'm not good that way. Besides, I'm kind of tired right now. Think I'll watch some TV." And he gets up from the table and walks into the other room.

Clearing the plates away, Reggie can't help but notice what a small amount Harmon has eaten and what a mess he's swirled the food into. She realizes that if Nicky had been playing with his food like that, she or Harm would have said something to him, stopped him from doing it.

But no one, she thinks, has said anything to Harmon about doing something a boy who was still in kindergarten knew better than trying.

And no one, she thinks, as she put the dishes into the suds, has said anything to her about what she has done, either.

She lets out her breath in a little explosion and plunges her hands into the hot soapy water.

Seventeen.

When she gets home from the bus stop that night, Reggie is glad she's remembered to run the special errand. Nicky has been watching for her from the front window and he greets her at the door, holding it open.

"What kind of friends did you get for Mr. Dumb? How many fish did you get him?"

She gives him a quick hug and tells him to hang on, that she has to get rid of her coat and the bags she is carrying.

"Can I see 'em, can I see 'em?" he pesters, impatient now. "Hey, Harmon. Wanna help us?"

"Looks like you've got plenty of help there already."

Reggie takes the white bag off the inner clear one, the one filled with water, where the three little fish are encased.

After looking into the tanks, she had told the man at the shop that she wanted some of the neons, please. When he'd asked her which kind, she'd told him, neon tetras. And he'd scooped out three of them, just as she'd requested. He'd tied a tight knot in the top of the bag, and asked her how long it would be until she'd be able to get them into their new home. She'd explained that she had only about fifteen minutes on the bus, and that she didn't have much of a walk from there, so it wouldn't be too long.

He'd nodded, given her the change, and then she'd been gone.

Nicky laughs at her efforts to unknot the bag. But she persists and finally undoes it. Reggie knows the temperature shouldn't be a shock, so she eases the whole bag down into the water to acclimatize the fish, to equalize their surroundings. "Let's let them stay in there, just for a while. By bedtime, we should be able to let them out of their little house."

Nicky seems content to watch the colourful fish. How they swim round and round in their world within another world. He is still looking in at them when Reggie announces supper.

"Well, Nick," Harmon asks, "have you figured out their names yet?"

Still chewing his food, Nicky looks thoughtful. When he has swallowed, he puts down his fork. "Yep. I'm going to call them Number Three, Number Four, and Number Five."

"Why no Number One and Number Two?"

Right away Nicky says to him, "You know we don't talk about those at table."

Hard to dispute that sort of logic. Though really, who still refers to it as Number Two and Number One? Must be the school, she thinks. History certainly repeats itself, doesn't it.

◆

Something is terribly wrong. Nicky is crying, shaking her, shaking her awake.

"They're spinning, they're spinning, they're going all in circles."

Reggie pulls herself out of sleep and tells him to climb into bed with her. That everything will be all right. That it was only a dream. She knows he's been having nightmares lately. She worries that they're genetic, that he's inherited them from her.

"No," he cries, "it's not a dream! It's Number Three and Four and maybe even Number Five. Something's bad wrong with them. They're swimming all funny."

She takes his hand and goes out to the other room and looks into the bowl with him. Nicky is right. There is something seriously out of whack with these new fish. She wonders if the guy at the shop had known they were sick. She remembers thinking he'd looked at her kind of strangely.

Nicky is crying and sounds really upset, and she turns on a brighter light so she can better see what is going on.

Mr. Dumb is almost smiling. He is not so dumb at all. That part she'd been right about. She was the dumb one.

Apparently goldfish think of neon tetras as sushi. Mr. Not-So-Dumb has spent the better part of the night doing fin-of-neon tetra appies.

One of the bright little red and blue fish is completely hopeless, barely moving, floating on its side at the top of the bowl. Another is pointed downward, mouth toward the bottom, lips still moving in futile O's, as if calling out for help. The third is swimming furiously in an endless circle. It reminds her in a sick way of the old race car slogan, "Go Fast, Turn Left, Go Fast, Turn Left." Only this guy isn't going to be winning any races.

"Oh, Nicky, I made a mistake," Reggie has to admit. "I must have gone and bought the wrong kind of fish. These weren't the right ones to be friends with Mr. Dumb. I feel so bad, Honey. I'm sorry."

Nicky is still crying, but watching closely – he seems almost hypnotized by the three tiny fish, swimming out their spooky dance of death. Then, without taking his eyes off them he says with a solemn face, "I know. It's okay, you didn't mean to do anything bad. Besides, they're only just some fishes." But she can tell by the sound of his voice that he is still crying, is feeling so very sad about it all.

Reggie picks up the bowl of water and carries it into the bathroom. The two of them look at each other, look at the fishbowl, look into the toilet, and as if they have already had an entire conversation, Nicky looks up at his mother and nods.

She takes this as a yes and dumps the water into the toilet, watching the whole lot of them, the pitiful tetras along with smart old Mr. Dumb, swim their way down the sides of their new porcelain world. Another nod from Nick and he solemnly pulls down the handle. And together they watch the fish disappear, swirling their way off to some other watery place.

Eighteen.

"A blind man came into the store today," says Reggie. This during the commercial. The three of them are watching TV.

"How did you know that he couldn't see?" Nicky asks, curious, his attention perked. "Didn't he have any eyes?" Ready for a ghoulish answer.

"Oh, he had eyes, all right. They were almost the colour of yours, but you could just tell that they didn't have anything going into them somehow. Kind of a blank look to them, I guess. I don't really know how to explain it."

"She knew a blind kid when she was about your age," interjects Harmon at this point.

Reggie is kind of surprised that he has remembered. He doesn't always seem to pay attention to the things she says. She even thinks she talks less now, tells him less because of that.

"Is that true, Mum? Did you really know a blind kid? How did he get blind? How did you play if he couldn't even watch TV with you?" Nicky seems to find this slightly amazing.

"Well, Honey, I don't know. It didn't seem hard at the time. Maybe we didn't watch TV so much when I was little."

"Well, what did you do then, anyways?" He is not about to be satisfied without an answer, even though the show has come back and Harmon has been lost to it.

"Gosh, we did lots of things. He was my very best friend. We saw each other nearly every day and I don't know – we just played. Oh, and we used to build forts in the living room of their house."

"Just like you and me used to? Back when I was little?"

"Yes, like when you were little. But, hey, now that you're so big and have important stuff to do like get up and go to school, maybe you better think about heading off to bed, eh?"

Nicky has always been good about going to bed. Reggie has stayed committed in her resolve to never use bed as a punishment. Maybe that's why he's never minded going there, even on a night like this, when it's starting to feel like summer, staying bright so much later, especially with the extra hour since they've gone back to Daylight Saving Time.

When she goes to tuck him in, she finds him lying with his eyes wide open, staring at the ceiling like some kind of corpse. He is moving one of his hands in front of his face and clearly making an effort not to follow it with his eyes. "Is this the way his eyes looked? The man in the store today? Open like this but not able to see anything?"

"Not exactly, Bud," she says and zooms her face down towards his. He blinks and squeals.

"Gotcha!" she says. "Just be glad that your eyes work so well. It's a lot easier than being blind."

Nicky looks thoughtful, still has more to say. "Sometimes it might be easier. Because if you were blind, you wouldn't have to look at yucky stuff. You wouldn't even have to close your eyes if you were scared."

"Well, now it's time to close your eyes, and the only thing scary here is me so, Boo. Good-night, eh." And she kisses him. "Love you."

As she closes the door, she hears his words, "Love you too."

◆

I am swimming underwater, but the water is so grey. It is hard to see anything, to even tell which way is up.

Even though I know it's water I'm in, I am able to breathe. Somehow the liquid feels sticky, but definitely breathable. The fluid seems richer than ordinary air. I realize I actually enjoy inhaling it.

My hair has grown much longer and is floating all around me. Suspended out around my head, like the sun's corona, it is like a mermaid's hair, beautiful. It feels like when I was small and could stretch out all the way in the bathtub. How I would lie there, listening to the gurgling underwater sounds, waiting for my mother to come and help me wash my hair, rinse it with vinegar to make it silky.

I can even smell the vinegar, sharp and acrid as I breathe, hurting almost, but in a good way, just a good little hurt.

But now there is something else here in the water with me, only I can't seem to see it, no matter how hard I look, no matter how wide I try to stretch my eyes open.

And then it is there, up close in front of me, too close. And I find that I can't breathe the water any more. I swallow, take in lungfuls, it is burning in my chest.

I can finally see it now, a slowly turning whitish thing. Something in formaldehyde, come loose from the bottom somewhere. Fetal crouched, it spins a loop, slower than a second hand, puts its scary face in mine, looks at me with empty eyes. Then I know it. See it clearly. It is Nicky.

Reggie is still feeling sick to her stomach at breakfast. Harmon offers her a piece of toast, but the sight of it gags her. She runs to the toilet, slams the door, makes terrible sounds.

Harmon finally comes to the door, knocks but doesn't open. Tells her he'll take Nick to school, let Gloria know she won't be in.

Reggie doesn't answer, only nods into the bowl.

Hears his steps moving back down the hall. Listens as he helps Nick gather up his gear. Nicky calls good-bye to her. She hears the bang of the outside door.

Rests her head along the rim, closes her eyes and shudders. Pukes another batch of bile and cries while it flushes down.

◆

Standing in the shower, she knows that this is not the same thing as a few unwanted pounds. Not a simple thickening around her hips and waist. This is also in her breasts. They are broad and heavy, trying to weigh her down. When she looks down, she can't see the orange of the hair between her legs. Even its brightness has been obstructed by the mound of growing flesh.

Reggie turns the water off, steps out and starts to dry. The mirror doesn't help her. She is past needing convincing. She knows she can't deny it any longer.

How many weeks has it been now, since her period? She doesn't like counting. Numbers seem so final.

She knows she should be happy. She knows that Harm will be.

But how is she supposed to know if it even belongs to him? It could just as easily turn out to be something left by Stu. Stu indeed, if that's how he spells it. What she is trapped in feels much more like a stew.

◆

Her uniform is getting tight, but everyone knows by now. Nicky is the one who seems the most excited. He keeps telling everyone he's going to get a brother. That a little brother will be better than a dumb old dog.

Reggie isn't sure of that, especially when she thinks about whose baby this might be. Only time will show who this critter is going to resemble. And she can't really remember anymore exactly what Stu had looked like, only knows he doesn't look even a little bit like Harmon.

When you got right down to it, she is embarrassed – what she remembers most is his rattlesnake tattoo. She would know that design if she ever saw it again, even though she might not recognize its owner. Reggie has a sudden and awful thought. She hopes that little brother won't come out pre-tattooed.

Nineteen.

There are only a few more weeks to go.

Not until the baby, but until she'll finish work.

This time she is bigger, even rounder than with Nicky. If she'd scared the customers that time, she must be terrifying them now. The store should pay her extra, she thinks, compensation to stay away. Bring back the customers, have a big sale. Reggie's safe at home. Though that sounded too much like baseball, Reggie Jackson. Call it the Mrs. October Sale.

Only this belly of hers doesn't look anything like a baseball, it's more like an Earthball. Maybe you better make that Mother Earthball.

◆

I am floating – no, more than floating, flying actually – over a field of flowers. I'm not high enough to feel afraid, even though I'm aware that I could fall at any minute.

Still, I'm high enough that it's impossible to identify the flowers. They might be roses, dandelions, or even clover. They form a cunning mix, impossible to know. Every colour dances as if caught in a steady breeze. The blossoms move, are in constant motion as I flutter above them. I am so surprised to feel this light, this supple.

A cloud begins to form in the distance, rises straight and fast, an upside-down tornado from the horizon. Then I see that it is no cloud. It is a wicked witch. She is flying on a broom, and when she comes close, I see that her face looks just like Harmon's. Only I know it isn't him, this wicked witch is a woman. Her teeth are very ugly, pointed on the ends. When I look at her more closely, I can see right through to her skull.

But as fast as she has flown here, she starts zooming away, spewing out a message like a skywriter across the clouds. This is no Surrender Dorothy, though it looks a lot the same. The string of words rests hanging there, dark black dust against the cloudy sky: Beware Violets.

Then like ash of fireworks, the message disintegrates. Falling toward the ground and onto me. I know I must be careful, not to let it touch my face, especially not to let it near my eyes.

With a jolt, Reggie wakes up.

Twenty.

Nicky is home from school with a cold. It isn't that bad, and Reggie knows she probably shouldn't have let him stay away, especially where he's now in the real business of it all – Grade One. Still, it's rainy, which always makes her feel lazier. Besides, where it's been a few days since her last day at work, the luxury of the time off is starting to set in. She and Nicky have played rounds of Slapjack 'til their hands have turned red, have even had one of their marathon games of War.

Later in the afternoon the two of them dress up and go out into the rain – probably not the best idea, considering his cold – but she is quick to justify all intakes of fresh air and walking these days. They are going to the video store to get themselves a movie, something they can laugh at and be rude to. Reggie's noticed that Nicky is especially skilled at this – good at making wisecracks off the cuff. She wonders where he gets this, how he's developed this skill. Harmon hardly ever makes jokes anymore and she doesn't remember Randy as being especially laugh-inducing.

The video store they go to is not their usual place, but it is closer to walk to than the big chain. Really, it is a pathetic collection, but what can you expect from a corner store.

They find one that fills the bill – it looks good and junky. She laughs as soon as she sees the one Nicky has selected, the image on its box something he's found irresistible. She knows it's not intended to be especially funny, that it's Grade-B science fiction, with a story she recalls as being completely implausible. When she helps him sound out the title, Nicky reveals he's already into the spirit of the game, renaming it *Nice Pirates* instead of *Ice Pirates*.

She is paying the woman behind the counter when a grey-haired man comes from the back room and into the main part of the store. Nicky steps behind her as if to conceal himself. She is easy to hide behind, big now as the Rocky Mountains on a summer day. When she turns to go, she sees that the man notices Nick. Gives him a look as if maybe he recognizes him, glances at Reggie, nods. Why does he have that funny look, she thinks, but turns and they go out the door.

Nicky is quiet as they walk down the street.

"What's the matter, Nick. Did that guy bug you?"

He seems reluctant to talk anymore. Mumbles something she can't quite hear.

"What did you say, Honey?"

"Nothing. I guess I thought he looked kind of scary. Like a scary guy from the movies. You know."

But just then the sun comes out, radiant from behind the clouds that have hung there all week, casting huge shadows on the sidewalk in front of them. Her shadow, especially, looms oversized, is enlarged by the line of her rain cape. Reggie spreads out her arms, magnifying the effect. "Arrrghh," she growls. "Look out, here comes the monster. Coming to get you. Better run home, little boy. Here I come, ready to get you."

And they both shriek their way home, full-out running all of the last block, Nicky yelling even louder than his silly mother.

◆

When they get to the house, and she can see his face, she realizes that he is more than just playing, that he is truly upset.

"Hey, Nick, I didn't mean to really scare you. That monster stuff was supposed to be a joke," pulling the cape up and over her head. "See, underneath it's still just me and little brother."

Nicky looks sheepish and twists his mouth. Says that he's sorry, that he just got too excited. Takes her hand, says that they should go and watch the movie.

But first, Reggie insists, they have to make the popcorn. Or no, because it's still daytime, maybe they better not. Probably instead, chips – chips with dip – will be even better.

◆

The movie had been pathetic, worse than Reggie'd remembered. Before it was even close to the end, they'd both decided to shut it off, calling it *Rice Pirates* after a particularly cheesy special effect.

"We could make a better movie," Reggie says while it rewinds. "*Monster Mother and Her Son* – rated PG, very PG – very pregnant, very scary."

Then she gets a better idea. "Wanna see the picnic movie Harmon made last summer? The one where all of us had the watermelon fight?"

While she looks through the videos, she thinks about the picnic. It was the silliest and most relaxed she'd ever seen Harmon be. The day had been hot and they were all planning to go for a swim anyway, so when the chunk of watermelon had fallen off her piece, she'd picked it off the ground and tossed it, "Hot Potato," hitting Nicky. From there, things had degenerated into total chaos. And all the while the camcorder, safely on its tripod, had recorded for posterity their sticky pink goofiness.

She wishes now that she'd done a better job of marking the video boxes. All of them look nearly the same. The labels, if there'd been any, are faded or hard to read. Finally, she picks one that looks like it says July, sticks it into the machine and hits the remote.

Right away she knows that this isn't the picnic. At least not the watermelon picnic. The person on the screen is the man they'd seen in the store. He's holding a whip in his hand and wearing a pair of tall leather boots. And he isn't wearing any other clothes.

Twenty-one.

Reggie has snapped off both the TV and the video and Nicky has gone running out of the room. She's seen enough, she thinks—though then again, maybe she hasn't. First, she knows, she has to check on Nick.

He is face down on his bed, kicking at the mattress, his body heaving with sobs. She hasn't seen him bawl this hard since he was a helpless baby. She sits on the edge of the bed and tries to comfort him. But when she tries to touch his head, he jerks away.

"Nicky, it's okay," she says, though she somehow knows it isn't. She also knows that eventually, she is going to have to go back and look at more of whatever is on that tape. But right now, her son is her only priority.

"Nicky, honey, I'm sorry. I didn't mean to put on the wrong movie. We probably already saw enough movies for one day."

When Nicky doesn't say anything, she reaches for him again. This time he permits her touch, and she begins to slowly rub between his bony shoulders, even though they're still bumping up and down with sobs. As she massages between the spots they've always called angel wings, she manages to gradually calm him. When it seems his crying has at last subsided, she asks, "Are you feeling sleepy, would you like a little nap?"

Nicky rolls over, turns his tear-streaked face to her and looks her in the eye: "I don't want to be alone. Let me come and be with you."

As Reggie starts to get up from the bed, Nicky reaches out and grabs so hard at her leg, she takes his hand in hers and sits down beside him again. It is hard to know what is going on behind that worried little face.

Then, as if hoping it might change everything, she puts on her brightest smile and suggests, "Why don't we go have ourselves a killer game of cards?"

He seems to hesitate, then smiles the tiniest crack of smile. "Okay, but only if I get to win."

"That's no fun!" She tugs at his arm and the two of them go out to sit at the table, underneath the silly-looking chandelier. While she gets the cards from the drawer, he turns on the lights. It isn't really dark enough, but Reggie isn't about to say no. Instead she just asks him, "Slapjack?"

"No way," he says. "I want War!"

◆

The only time she gets up from the table is to get them both a glass of juice. The only sounds, aside from the occasional grunt of satisfaction or loud cry of "Yesss!" are the steady snap of cards and the sweep of the pile to one side or the other.

Finally they both hear the truck pull into the driveway. And that's their cue to stop. Harmon is home from work. They hear the engine quit, hear the heavy *ka-thump* of the truck door banging shut.

Hear his key turning in the latch of the front door. Hear the thud of his shoes as he drops them, *bump, bump*. Hear the creak of the floor as he walks towards the kitchen, calling. "Reggie? Nick?" Just once.

When he comes into the room, he asks what the two of them are doing, as their game has clearly gone into pause mode. Asks whether he's interrupting something important, then just as quickly heads down the hall, pulls the bathroom door closed firmly behind him. The sound of the shower seems to unfreeze both of them. "I better start us some supper, Nicky boy. How's about you help by cleaning up the cards?"

Not a peep of argument, no whining about their game not being finished, who the winner will be. He gathers the cards, raps them against the table squaring them into a pile, slips the elastic around them and puts them into the drawer. He sidles over to Reggie and asks if he can set the table, help her get things ready some way.

◆

If their supper is quieter than usual, Harmon doesn't seem to notice. If anything, his appetite seems immense, as he takes seconds, then finishes off the Hamburger Helper she's made, scraping the last of the noodles directly from the pan. Reggie and Nicky exchange a few small looks, then as if on a signal, they get up from the table, excuse themselves to other things.

Reggie goes to the closet and pulls out the bag that still holds the pieces of sweater. It seems like a good time to get going on it again. She knows that it will give her something to do, a nice distraction. The sleeves are already done, and so is one of the fronts. When she holds up the part she's left off on, the back, she's washed in disappointment. Barely an inch of knitted rows are gathered on the needle. The piece looks barely begun. Nicky's brought out crayons, the tablet he calls his art book, and sets into serious scribbling on something unrecognizable.

When Reggie asks him what he's drawing, he tells her that it's what blind people see. And just as fast, he asks her back, "What are you making with all that string you're twisting up?"

"I'm knitting a sweater for Harmon. It was supposed to be a surprise. Only now I guess it won't be."

Nicky looks back down at his tangle of colour and carries on swirling, two crayons at a time. "Maybe blind people are kind of lucky."

"And why's that?"

"They get to see whatever they want."

Just then, Harmon walks into the room. "Isn't anybody gonna watch any TV with me tonight?"

"I think it's time for my bath and bed." And with that, Nicky gathers his crayons, closes his book, and heads down the hallway.

"Wow, I guess you were right to keep him home, Reggie. The kid really is sick with something."

"Yeah, Harm, I guess he is. With something."

◆

When Harmon heads for bed, Reggie makes an excuse, says that she has a few things to do, will be there in a while. Thinks to herself how wildly unobservant he is, to not even notice the growing sweater on her lap. And how lucky that he hasn't noticed the video she's left in the machine.

Once she hears his quiet snore, she tiptoes to the television, hits the VCR's on-button and pops out the afternoon's tape. She decides to put it away in the same spot where she's been keeping the sweater all these months. If the side shelf in her closet has been a safe enough place to hide a gift, it will be safe enough to hide this, something much more important.

Twenty-two.

Over the next few days, Reggie takes whatever private time she can make to scour her way through the shelves of videotapes. Most of them are unmarked and filled with stupidities. Ironically, a lot of them hold *America's Funniest Home Videos*. She remembers something she's heard about Bob Saget, the oh-so-wholesomely presented actor who serves as the show's family-guy host. In spite of looking like the geeky boy who lives next door, his live performances are supposed to be anything but wholesome – apparently, he is known for some of the foulest jokes in stand-up. She reminds herself: You just can't tell by looking, can you.

And all the while she keeps adding rows to the nubby brown body of the sweater. She understands why she'd left off where she had. The back section is so wide, it's easy to get discouraged. At least the rows have now grown enough to finally prompt Harmon to ask what she is making. He doesn't seem very pleased at the prospect of a cardigan. Still, she'd done her best to smile back sweetly, promised that once it was finished, it would look much better.

Reggie drags the sweater along to whichever room her search takes her, a kind of constantly-growing security blanket. If Harmon were suddenly to arrive home, she knew she could hide whatever she might have been doing by picking up the knitting again. The scratchy wool also gives her something to do while she speeds on fast-forward through the many unmarked tapes, and she wonders why she hasn't been able to grow the sweater this easily before.

When she discovers a tape with an out-of-focus child on it, the shock is almost electrical. Automatically, she hits both the off and eject buttons. She pulls the cassette from the machine and holds it in her hand, realizing that this puts a whole new twist on her cataloguing. Men with boots and whips are one thing – children quite another.

As she heads towards her hiding spot in the closet, she decides she isn't going to take a chance on Harmon or Nicky walking in on her while she watches this one. She'll save it for a time when she can be sure she is alone. Or maybe she'll just hide it away, until she better understands what exactly she should do.

◆

It seems hard to believe, but her belly just keeps on getting bigger. It's a good thing she's been able to leave the store. It's uncomfortable to stand now for any length of time. Her groin pinches almost steadily with the weight of the baby so low. Although she sometimes feels close to crying from the ache at the top of her thighs, she smiles silently at the thought that the part is misnamed – that it should be called groan, not groin.

Still, she pulls herself out of bed every morning, sees to it that Nicky eats at least some toast and peanut butter before he heads off for the day. She is grateful that Harm has adjusted his schedule to be able to drop Nicky off, as she can barely manage the walk over to the school anymore. Meeting him at the end of the day is about all that she can manage. Her afternoon walk over to the school is now when she finally gets dressed. Otherwise, she spends nearly all her time draped in sloppy nightgowns. She even hates doing up the belt on her robe.

She knows she won't have too many more days left to herself, that soon she'll likely be going into labour. At last week's appointment, the doctor had told her again that, even though she hasn't gone full term, the baby might decide to come at any time. But, she tells herself, she isn't going to have any baby today. Today, she has some viewing ahead of her. Because, now that she's hit pay dirt, she wants one more lookie-look in case there might be more tapes to add to the pair she has hidden in the closet.

◆

Nicky is home from school again, only this time he really is sick. It started in the night, with him coming in to wake her, complaining about his tum. When she'd padded along to the bathroom with him, almost immediately he'd leaned into the toilet, thrown up more food than Reggie could imagine him eating in a day. She had long since put the Halloween candy away, so knew it hadn't been that temptation that had brought this on.

He'd sat down on the floor, looked up at her in sweaty relief, "That's a lot better already." Then promptly spewed out another round of sticky vomit, this time onto his jammies and the floor. So much for the initial good catch, she'd thought, while she ran a shallow bath for him and went to get him something clean and warm.

As she'd settled him back into bed, she'd placed a towel beside his pillow and put an ice cream bucket on the floor – explaining, "just in case."

◆

Because Harmon knows that Nicky is sick, he heads off to work early. Early enough to miss the jack-hammering crew of city workers who pick a spot in front of their house to do some exploratory surgery. Of all the days for a noisy job, thinks Reggie, a day when Nicky needs to be able to rest.

But apparently the racket doesn't bother him, as he just keeps on sleeping through the intermittent digging. Finally, when it's nearly eleven, Reggie decides she better shake him awake, see how he's doing, whether he wants to try eating.

He seems groggy, but willing enough to sample some ginger ale and crackers. He even gets out his art book and crayons, and works for a long time on a picture for Reggie. When he shows her, she isn't sure, but asks anyway, "A giraffe?"

"Yep."

"That's a good picture, Nicky. You even gave him a tree so he'd have something to eat. But what made you think of drawing that?"

"I think I'd like to be a giraft."

"That's a strange one. How come?"

"They're taller than everybody else, and they don't have to say anything because they can't talk."

"How do you know that?"

"I don't know. I just know it."

"But if you couldn't talk, how would you say things like I love you or – if you were a giraffe, how would you say Trick or Treat?"

"I'd be big enough, they'd just see me and know what I wanted."

Hard to dispute that kind of logic, Reggie thinks, and asks if Nicky wants to go for a snuggle and maybe another rest. Amazingly, he agrees without any fuss.

◆

Having him home makes it complicated for Reggie to look at the next batch of tapes. She is getting sick of fast-forwarding through baseball games or late-night infomercials. Still, when he seems to be sleeping soundly, armed with her now nearly-complete sweater-back, she turns to the videos again, making sure the volume is muted.

The first one she tries is a bingo. It shows a young girl, dressed in a long flowing cape. The only other thing she has on is a dog-collar. It takes a minute, but despite the Goldilocks wig, Reggie recognizes her – the girl who bought the cigarettes. The eyes are the same, but not tuned to their usual fierceness. Instead, despite their heavy make-up, they are dull and gaga-looking.

She seems to be following commands, occasionally looking off to the left, as if towards someone who is speaking. When she moves in a jerky circle, skipping, Reggie can see that the collar is attached to a leash, and that the leash seems to be fixed to a point in the floor. The girl then stops, appears to be listening again, then holds up her hands like little paws, lets her tongue hang out sloppily, doggy-panting. When the command orders the girl to sit, Reggie turns it off, knowing she's already seen too much. Pops it out and tucks it into her space in the bedroom closet.

◆

She looks in on Nicky again, adjusts the covers and gives him a kiss. He murmurs a happy cooing sound while he sleeps, her big baby bird.

The one place she hasn't yet looked is the shop in the garage.

Like so many other garages, this one doesn't seem to have ever been used for its original purpose. Harmon has his workshop out here, a bench where he works on projects of one sort or another. Even the dull concrete floor shows no evidence of oil or other clues that a car has ever been housed here.

Reggie pokes around in the cupboards beneath the counter, puzzles over what some of the objects even are. Then kneels down on the floor, with the sweater beside her. She lifts the lid of the shining metal toolbox, admires the orderly mix of tools arranged there. Then raises the accordioned shelf that makes her think of her Gramma's sewing box. It squeaks a little protest but rises enough to reveal an array of tapes. They look to be arranged as neatly as if placed there by a librarian.

But suddenly she realizes she isn't alone. She's been so busy trying to convince herself of what she is seeing, she hasn't heard him open the door and step inside the tidy room. Just hears the thick inhale of air that he takes, hears him ask in a tone that she knows is too quiet what the hell she is doing.

"You're home early," Reggie offers. "I never heard your truck."

"There's some kind of goddamn roadwork out there. The driveway's blocked with whatever they were doing, so I had to park on the street. But I asked you Reggie, what the hell are you *doing*?"

She hears her own voice again, the sound of it like from a ventriloquist standing far away. "I know why you wanted the video camera."

And then how he explodes into a stream of rage, into a thundering bellow from hell. Reggie feels the weight of his ring smash against her cheekbone, hears the crunching sound in her face, the spring of her neck as she falls against the floor. Feels the bulk of the sweater being shoved into her mouth. Tries to scream through it, feels herself choking on its loosened strings. Sees him fold down the shelf in the tool box, close the lid, then heft the red box off the floor as he heads for the door. His parting shot, "Harmon's gotta fix a few things" does not leave her comforted.

◆

She must have passed out, but can't tell for how long. The room isn't dark, but the light from the high little window is different than before. Someone is touching her face, tugging at the sweater, trying to pull it from her mouth. She can hear crying, and the repeated "Mudgie," a name she hasn't heard since Nicky was two.

Reggie tries to reach for him, but her arm isn't working. The other one seems pinned beneath her somehow. A terrible sound comes out of her. "Wuuuunnn."

Nicky covers his ears and cries harder, his face a mix of fear and trying to understand. But then he looks up, sees the doorway, Harmon outlined there, a hammer dangling from his hand. Suddenly, he knows what Reggie is trying to tell him to do. He stands and, as he scoots for the door to the kitchen, Reggie notices how short on his legs the pirate pyjamas are.

Harmon wings the hammer toward Nicky and connects. For an instant, Nicky looks ready to fly, as he seems to be lifted from the ground. Just as quickly, he crumples backwards. Reggie's throat closes around an impossible cry as he slumps downward, a suddenly deflated bag. She hears the horrid *clunk-clunk* as his head and the hammer hit the unforgiving floor. Blood streams immediately from his ear.

There isn't enough air in the room to scream or call out. "Ambudanz," is the best she can do. "Get ambudanz." She turns onto her side, does her best to crawl to him, the rough concrete biting at her skin, while a series of hoarse moans, inhuman as a siren, rise from inside her. "Ambudanz...."

And then Harmon is standing above her, straddling her waist, speaking in a seethingly ugly voice, "I suppose you've been looking in cupboards and drawers."

He places one foot on her chest, uses his boot to roll her onto her back, then pauses – as if to make a list of all the things he wants to say. "I bet you've been thinking how smart you are, sneaking around behind my back like a spy." As he speaks, he yanks at the sweater with both hands, ripping the fabric of it, unraveling clumps of wool. He hurls the bits down onto her like horrid fuzzy snow, punctuating the words he spits at her. "So, what did you find – body parts? No. A few magazines? Some video tapes. Nobody was hurt, Reggie. Nobody."

He pauses again.

She can hear his breathing, coming through his mouth, heavy and panting, like an animal. "Not until now. And now – well, you can see what's happened." Tears begin to run down his face. He scowls like a baby and his voice cracks. "All of this is your fault, Reggie. I want you to remember that. All of this is your fault and you have to pay."

He wipes his nose on his sleeve. "Maybe I can make you pay. Maybe, finally I can even give you the kind of fuck you've always wanted." And with that, he grabs the hammer from the floor, wraps his terrible claw of a hand around the business end. Reggie screams as loud as she can, feels him pull at her legs, shove the hard wooden handle up and into her, *pump pump pump* and then the mercy of blackness.

Twenty-three.

The fire crew are the ones who find her. Somebody has been a good Samaritan and phoned for help. Heard something terrible in their neighbourhood, had the sense and the guts to phone 9-1-1.

By the time they arrive, the baby has mostly gushed its way out. An instinctual reaction from her body. A bloodied lifeless grey thing on the previously immaculate floor.

The prick of the IV going into her arm brings Reggie slightly around. A sea of police and paramedics fill the room. When she lifts her head to see what's going on, a cool hand touches her forehead, holds her down. A voice whispers, "There, there, you're going to be all right."

And when they lift the baby so they can cut the cord, she has just enough strength to indicate she wants to look at him.

A paramedic cradles the baby, holds the infant towards her, says quietly, "It's a boy," then moves in close enough for her to see him better. Even with the man's big hand protecting the top of the tiny head, she can tell that the skull is caved in. Despite the tragically lopsided face, she can see that he's Harmon's son, that he has the same square line to his little jaw. His eyes look so tightly shut, as if he never wants to see the things that go on in this life.

And who could blame him.

Through the gloss of her tears, she can see her precious Nicky, sprawled on the once-pristine surface, a shape gathered around him like a snow angel made from blood. Above him a police officer, yellow stripe blurring up the side of his dark blue pants, holds a notebook in his hand, is shaking his head as he writes.

When they move her onto the low gurney, she asks whether she can say good-bye to Nicky. They roll her near him, help her dangle her arm close enough that she can touch his face. Allow her to touch the skin of his cheek, feel the way it is already too cool. When finally she nods, they strap her in place, roll her into the night, out the now-open garage doors, down the driveway toward the waiting vehicle. She can see a small knot of nervous looking neighbours, wonders which one of them might have made the call. Feels herself being lifted inside the ambulance, then drifts off again, to some hopeless dark place where the only sound is the song of sirens and speed.

Postscript.

Sometimes, late at night, the rain is so hard it wakes me. I lie in bed, breathing quietly as I can, just so I can listen to it. I love the way it sometimes comes in waves, in a rush upon the land, harder and then easier, the way a woman's body moves in the labour of birthing.

Sometimes I want to run outside and feel it on my skin. Feel it soak all the way through my clothes and deep into all of the pores of me. Maybe that would clean me out. Maybe that would do it.

When the rains come so hard, and it is always in the night, I wonder who might be out there, getting wet from it. Are they running, are they holding still, hugging themselves under the ledge of somebody's eaves? And are they getting themselves cleaned out, soaked to the skin and made new again?

◆

February 28, 2011

Nicky's birthday. Not just would be, should be Nicky's birthday.

Still is. Always will be.

They say you change your skin every seven years. That you get a whole new set of it, everywhere. When I think about a new set of skin, I picture one of those baby sleepers, the kind with the built-in feet. Something you could just step into and it would fit, the way a hermit crab finds a bigger shell when he needs a new place to live.

But would a new suit of skin mean you'd get to change who you are? Would it make you a different person from who you were before? A chance to start over, do it all again? Only this time, do it different, do it better. Shrink down any troubles you'd had the first time around, shrink them to where you could fold them up, tuck them into your pocket, maybe forget them altogether.

It's been a couple of new suits of skin since all of this happened, but I still don't feel like a different person. In some ways it's hard to believe it's been such a long time. Other times, it seems like it was just last week. Even so, I'm probably still too full of questions.

Oh, I learned what happened afterwards. Nothing too surprising. Harmon found himself a way of fixing things up so he wouldn't have to face the music. Vain to the end, he stuck his video camera on its tripod, and rigged up a scenario that would see him out in style. Wore his fancy open-fly panties, showed his little weenie. Rigged a trigger, blasted the head off of it just as the rifle took his brain. One thing about that Harmon, he was good at figuring things out.

As for me, the pain's not so intense anymore. Heck, my hair's not even so orange. Of course, I'm still looking for that new set of skin, the chance to start over, be a whole brand-new person. A new self every seven years – if only.

Nicky still had a couple of months until he would have turned seven. Now, a couple of skin changes later, he'd be taller than me, would be a man.

Sometimes I can go outside myself, can look at all that happened, view it like some Friday night horror movie the channel changer got stuck on. But why I was the one to live through it all, I've never been able to figure.

When I look in the mirror, sometimes I dream. Squint so that this mark on my face doesn't even show. Squint so hard that sometimes I see Nicky there beside me. Always, he is smiling, making one of his jokes. On other days, it's like I can see nothing at all. As if the mirror is tarnished, has nothing to reflect.

But please, I apologize. As always, I diverge.

Of course, there was an inquest, though it felt more like a trial. How could a mother not know about something so horrible, going on right under her nose, in her own home?

It's not a good excuse, but the world was different then. We weren't attached by cell phones, didn't have Facebook or amber alerts.

Turns out that there were dozens of the videos. No feature length extravaganzas, just nasty little homemade movies, some only half-a-minute or so. Quickies. As it turned out, he'd hidden them just about everywhere. In the toolbox, in the truck, even a few in his locker at the store – edited, classified, labelled for the world. Good planning, Mr. Harmon. Here we have Exhibits A, B, C and D. Nice work, though hardly *America's Funniest*.

Nicky was in some of them. Other kids, the few of them they could find, lived in the area, not far from our house. And of course, there was the little girl with the messy hair, only no one ever found her. There were the others too, ones that no one knew. Oh yeah, and the weird guy from the back of the corner store. At least they managed to find him, and when they rounded him up, they threw away the key.

Harmon was in a few of them. But even when he wasn't, there it was – the inside of the truck. Also the little room with the porthole out the back. There were zoom shots of kids playing on the school grounds, then close-ups of what must have been Harmon whacking his meat. It's amazing how the right degree of zoom can enhance an undersized cock.

The worst ones of course, were the ones with Nicky in them. I learned what happened that weekend they went fishing. The same night I was having myself some adult-style sex, my son was getting some of the same, but without any of the joy, and in the back of a truck.

Other ones were shot in other places, even in our bed. Nicky with a glassy face, stoned on something or other, lying there, spread out like a bird against the sky.

I can't help think about times when I came home late from work. Just a beer or a glass of wine with Sylvia or one of the girls. Harmon watching TV, Nicky asleep in his bed. Probably sleeping off a dose. How could I have not known? How could I have been so goddamn blind.

As for my poor baby with no name, he lives always in my mind. I sometimes even see that grey little face. I think of how he grew, floating all those months inside my body. And how hard he could kick – how his tumbling in my belly used to make Nicky laugh and laugh. I think about the good times all of us could have had, what fun life might have been with a brother for Nicky. And though I think about him and imagine him – the one we always called little brother – it's not the same way I remember my darling Nicky.

Nicky, the one who should be here today, standing tall, making his way in the world. This world that can be so terrible, but the same world that can be so full of wonder and joy.

When I think of Nicky, I remember hugs and card games and hot chocolate on a snowy day – all the small unremarkable things that make the world so remarkable.

Acknowledgements

With thanks to Jane Barker Wright, whose early encouragement made me persist with Reggie's story. To participants of the Writer's Retreat Group at Matsqui Penitentiary (in particular, Penny Duane) whose gentle feedback carried me forward with the work. To Luciano Iacobelli, who made me turn things inside out. And of course to George, the man who helps me keep my crazy life in balance.

Other Quattro Novellas